NEPHIL
The Seventh Day Se
By Leslie Swartz

Copyright 2019, Leslie Swartz

Library of Congress Control Number: 2020903738

ISBN: 9781697004052

The pain of parting is nothing to the joy of meeting again.
Charles Dickens

Prologue

King Gevar paced the floor, the Mead Hall empty but for him. He grew impatient, his spies having told him of Chief Thryme's plan to invade nearly a month before. He downed a cup of ale, but it did little to calm his nerves.

Light poured into the room as the door swung open, making it difficult to see the man stepping inside. As the king's eyes adjusted, he was relieved to see the blacksmith edging closer, dragging a wagon overflowing with swords.

"You've done it!" he exclaimed. "I didn't believe it possible! How did you manage to create so many Ulfberhts in only a month's time?"

"I don't sleep," the man replied.

The king laughed and poured him a drink. "Come! I can think of no one more deserving of a pint than you."

He took the cup with no intention of imbibing its contents and nodded politely. "Thank you." The king offered him a leather purse heavy with coins, but he refused it. "I require no payment. Only the assurance that you will do everything in your power to keep your people safe."

"But I *must* pay you," Gevar insisted, inspecting the weapons. "These are impeccable. The work you put into them merits reward. If not coin, what would you have as compensation?"

"I need nothing," he claimed, his voice stern. It was then that the king noticed how piercing the man's azure eyes were through wisps of blond hair, striking as they seemed to look right through him. The blacksmith turned to go. "I should be getting home."

"Wait," Gevar commanded. "If you will not take silver, you must at least honor me by attending my daughter's wedding tomorrow. It will be here at sunset. You shall be my guest." The man thought for a moment, tightening the strap around the hammer that hung from his belt before nodding in agreement and taking his leave.

Hodr came upon a buck drinking peacefully from the stream, oblivious to the hunter and his intention. He pulled back on his bow, but before he could release the arrow, the snapping of branches startled him and the deer, which sprinted off, unharmed. Laughter wafted through the air from behind and as he turned, his annoyance turned to joy.

"Nanna," he greeted, a wide smile brightening his face.

"Beloved," she beamed, hurrying toward her betrothed. She flung her arms around his neck and kissed him sweetly.

"What are you doing here? Shouldn't you be preparing?"

"I will," she said. "I just *needed* to see you." She kissed him again, her skin warm with desire as she ran her hands over his chest before untying her cloak.

"What are you doing?" he asked, looking around for intruders.

"Just offering a taste of what's to come," she teased, opening her cloak to reveal the smooth, alabaster form underneath.

"Someone could see us."

"These are your family's private hunting grounds. No one will find us here," she reassured him, pawing at his belt.

"Your father would kill me."

"He wouldn't dare break his only daughter's heart the day before her wedding. Tomorrow, we'll be married, expected to start providing heirs to my father's throne. This is the only chance we have for it to just be about us." She took his hand and placed it on her backside, pressing her body to his. "Be with me."

He relented, grabbing her tightly and kissing her hard. As he struggled to get his trousers down, they were interrupted by an unnatural-sounding growl.

"Who's there?" Hodr called into the forest. Nanna covered herself quickly, her strawberry locks whipping in the cool autumn wind as they both scanned the woods for signs of life. They heard the odd snarling again, but couldn't place where it was coming from. Hodr readied his bow.

"It's only me," a voice called from beyond the trees. Slowly, a figure emerged from the shadows.

"Baldr?" Nanna asked. "I hardly recognize you. What happened to your face?"

He looked pale, gaunt, and sickly, not like the man that disappeared several months before.

"This man," Baldr said, slamming his hand to his chest as he stepped closer. "Has complicated feelings when it comes to you."

"You know this person?" Hodr asked.

"I used to," she admitted. "His uncle is the chief of the village across the lake. My father had arranged a marriage between us to keep the peace, but--"

"She found him to be brutish and lacking in proper hygiene," Baldr huffed, his voice sounding pained and raspy, not at all how Nanna remembered it.

"Why do you refer to yourself in the third person?" Hodr wondered.

"I refer to *this*," Baldr replied, again banging on his chest. "The one you call 'Baldr'."

"You should see a wound-healer," Nanna told him. "You're not making sense."

"Get behind me," Hodr instructed.

"What? Why?"

"Do it, Nanna," he commanded as he lifted his bow. "I do not think this creature is human."

"Guilty," the demon inside Baldr confirmed. "See, I only wanted to rape and pillage, but Baldr here has an intense desire to hurt the woman that broke his heart. He's just in here," he complained, pounding on the side of his head with his fist. "Screaming at me to do my worst. He wants death to come to you slow and bloody and he wants to feel these hands do the work of it. I will get no peace until it's done." He rushed toward the couple and as Nanna scurried behind her fiance, Hodr pulled back on his bow, releasing an arrow directly into the demon's heart. Baldr fell, a strange, black shadow peeling away from him as he hit the ground. The frightened lovers fled into the woods, afraid that whatever had left him would attach itself to one of them next.

That evening, Thryme, along with several of his most trusted soldiers, stormed into King Gevar's Mead Hall where preparations were underway for Nanna's wedding. He carried the body of his slain nephew on his shoulders until he reached the king's table where he slammed it down in grief and rage.

"Where is Hodr?!" he demanded. "Do not hide him from me. I will have vengeance!"

"Is that Baldr?" the king asked. "What's happened?"

"Hodr, the one you allow to defile your daughter, put an arrow through his heart. This will not go unpunished."

"Are you sure it was Ho--"

"Of course I'm sure!" Thryme shouted through his full, auburn beard. "I have spies everywhere. Now, give him to me!"

"I don't know where he is. He will be here tomorrow for the wedding. I'll question him then."

"There will be a wedding here tomorrow, but it will not be his," Thryme asserted. "If you wish to maintain peace between our lands, you have one choice. *I* will marry Nanna. She will give me sons, heirs to unite our people. Should she refuse, this time tomorrow, I will burn your village and every living thing in it to the ground."

King Gevar stood in stunned silence as Thryme lifted the corpse from the table and carried it back outside. His men followed, some glancing back at the king in derision, one even spitting on the floor. Gevar looked up toward his daughter's private room where he could see her peeking her head out, tears streaming down her lightly freckled cheeks.

5

The day of the wedding came. Guests filled the seats, ale flowed and the air smelled of roasting boar. The blacksmith peered into the hall, taking note of Thryme's men stationed on either end of the king's table. He turned to see Hodr walking confidently to the building.

"Are you suicidal?" the blacksmith asked, standing in the young man's way.

"I am not afraid of Chief Thryme or of his men," Hodr proclaimed. "I am to be married today."

"I see. You do not wish to die, you're simply an imbecile. Apologies." He slammed his large fist down on the top of Hodr's head, knocking him out cold. He then pulled the boy's tunic over his face and carried him over his shoulder into the building and up the stairs to Nanna's room. She was startled as the blacksmith dropped her fiance onto the bed and held his finger to his lips. "Stay here," he told her. "No matter what you hear, do not open this door. Do you understand?" The girl nodded, rushing to close the door behind the man as he left.

Thryme entered the hall, arrogance and body odor following him like sheep. The crowd stilled as they waited, all relieved, if not somewhat saddened to see Nanna descend from the stairs. She was as beautiful as she'd ever been, her soft hair flowing down her back, a silver bridal crown resting on her head. Her cheeks appeared flushed and her small but shapely frame was draped in the finest of fabrics. She approached her would-be husband, staring at him with such intensity that he began to feel uncomfortable.

"Nanna," he said. "You look lovely. I don't remember your eyes being so--" There was a thud between them. The two looked down to see a hammer lying on the floor, just beneath Nanna's dress. Thryme picked it up and handed it to her. "You dropped this," he said, confused. "From your... lap?"

"It was on my belt," she corrected.

"You're not wearing a--"

She brought the hammer back and swung it so hard into Thryme's face that it came out the back of his head. He fell to the floor, blood and brain spilling onto the large wooden planks. The berserkers rushed her and as they pulled their weapons, Nanna's appearance suddenly shifted from that of a young girl on her wedding day to that of the tall, muscular blacksmith. The man fought off three of the soldiers with his hammer, killing them with single blows to the head. As wedding guests fled, he seemed to create bolts of lightning from thin air and wield them as weapons, making light work of slaughtering the rest of Thryme's men.

As the smoke cleared, one man who had remained seated finished the last of his ale and began to clap. "Well done, brother," he said as he stood.

"Lucifer?"

"They call me 'Loki' here. It means 'lock'. I thought it somewhat fitting."

"Why are you here?" the blacksmith asked.

"Why am I ever anywhere? A demon got loose, so I came to fetch it. Turns out, it's been handled for me. Thryme, however, was a mess I should have cleaned up long ago. I appreciate your assistance, though I would have managed. Why are *you* here?"

"I came to protect this village from a maniac and his blind followers. I provided arms to the king in the hopes of avoiding spilling any blood myself, but after thinking on it, I decided it was too risky. Thryme was too dangerous. What did he have to do with you?"

"When his mother was pregnant with him, she became possessed," Lucifer explained. "I removed the demon, but the woman didn't survive. I should have left the child to die, as well. He'd been corrupted, his mind altered. But, I was weak and couldn't bear it. I thought, given time and a proper influence, the boy could overcome his less desirable instincts. So, I tore him from his mother's rotting womb and delivered him to his father. I've wondered for decades if I'd made the right decision. Clearly, I did not."

"I can hardly fault you for saving the life of an infant, Lucifer."

"Perhaps *you* can't, but no doubt our Father's been most disappointed in me."

"I doubt that," the blacksmith said, putting his arm around his brother. "Do you know how many times I've strayed from God's plan because I felt sorry for humans? Thousands. God still loves *me* and I'm not even His favorite. There is nothing you could do that He wouldn't forgive."

"I appreciate you saying that. Thank you, Barachiel."

The brothers left the Hall, closing the doors behind them. They didn't seem to notice King Gevar cowering under a table, not ten feet from where they'd been talking or Nanna and Hodr spying from above. Gevar rose and looked to his daughter, who now stood at the top of the stairs, quivering in fear and disbelief. The king clutched his chest, his hands and voice trembling as he said, his voice barely loud enough for the others to hear, "The man with the hammer...he controls the thunder."

Chapter 1

Lucifer's eyes slowly opened as he took back control of the body he'd abandoned nearly three years earlier. His amazement at the fact of its availability turned to anger when he realized how the feat had been accomplished.

He pulled the oxygen mask from his face and choked, his esophagus burning as he gingerly removed the feeding tube from his throat. The satin sheet beneath him was stained and smelled of old sweat as did his clothes, the same slacks and button-down he'd been wearing when he left. The garishly decorated room felt familiar, though he couldn't quite place it. He felt lightheaded as he sat himself up, noticing his arm connected by needle and tube to two bags, one filled with saline and the other brimming with his own blood. He extracted the needles, his skin repairing the small punctures left behind. He threw back the blanket to reveal another disturbing discovery; he'd been cathed. His lips pursed and a low growl escaped his larynx as he removed the device, the sharp pain enraging him further. His body felt weak as he stood and pulled his pants up, his eyes adjusting to the dim light that peeked through dark curtains. He saw four men lying on cots opposite the ornate poster bed he'd been in. They, too, were on breathing machines, unconscious and joined to IV bags similar to his. He recognized them as host bodies of some of the demons that had attacked him and his siblings in Gabriel's apartment. As he opened the door to the next room, a throne sitting at one end, bottles and paraphernalia littering tables and floor, he realized he knew exactly where he was. He seethed, "Allydia Cain."

"Lilith was a distraction," Lucifer growled, pushing past Valerie, stumbling into her apartment and dropping himself onto her sofa.

"You look like shit," she commented, closing the door. "And smell worse."

"Good to see you, too, sister."

"What are you doing here? Aren't you supposed to be in Hell, torturing people and shit?"

"I don't torture souls," he corrected. "That's a myth. Hell isn't what I think you think it is."

"Whatever. Why do you look like you just got done with six rounds of chemo?"

"It seems the vampire queen was keeping this body as an on-demand food source while I was away. Remind me to wring that foul creature's neck next time I see her."

"Jesus."

"I wish you people wouldn't use that name as a way of conveying astonishment. It's very confusing. As for why I'm here, tell me, have you had any visions lately?"

"Just personal stuff like when I was in high school. Nothing important since you chucked Lilith back in her hole."

"Well, that's disappointing," he complained. "Perhaps you need a jump start."

She backed away. "The fuck you mean?"

"Like a car battery. Just a little boost." He rushed her, grabbing her head and transferring memories to her, hoping they would trigger a related premonition. He knew she'd be cross with him, but he was desperate.

Her eyes grew wide as she was overwhelmed by information, the horrors of Hell flooding her mind, the despair of the damned like a weight on her chest.

"I hope that wasn't too unpleasant," he said, letting go and stepping aside as she staggered toward the couch. "You must understand the urgency." She nearly collapsed, but caught herself, unwilling to sit, instead turning back to her brother, rage twisting her features. She marched toward him, gaining strength with every step. He sighed, resigned to the coming punishment.

She punched him in the nose. "This is why I can't stand you!"

"Apologies," he said, realigning his broken nasal bones as they began to heal and wiping away the blood with the sleeve of his shirt. "But I need to know where to begin my search. That thing you saw is more dangerous than Lilith. He doesn't want to rule over humans; he wants to end them."

"Just close the Gate," she condescended. "Demons get sucked back in. Problem solved."

"Demons, yes. But what I'm hunting is something else entirely. He was an angel of the highest order, tasked with gathering the materials of the Earth that God would use to create the first humans. He was a devoted servant of the Almighty and watched over our Father's new creatures as a sort of guardian. This was, of course, before Barachiel was blinked into existence. He cared for God's people like pets, tending to their needs when they could not. Teaching them how to hunt, showing them which plants were safe for consumption, and providing comfort to them when they were hurt. He was kind to them. One might go as far as to say that he loved them. But, when the first son of man killed his brother, the angel was horrified. He never truly got over it."

"Are you talking about Cain and Abel?" Valerie asked. "That was *real*?"

"Indeed. As the humans multiplied and had their inevitable conflicts and the bodies of the murdered grew to be many, the angel became enraged. He was livid that he'd had a part in constructing such sadistic creatures. He used dark magic to bind himself, permanently, to the Earth and vowed not to rest until every human had been wiped from it. He used an army of locusts to destroy crops, starving a country's residents. When he became impatient, he cursed entire continents with plague. God was furious, so He fashioned Perdition, a literal bottomless pit made using Earth's magnetic field, and tossed the angel in. Later, Hell was created around that pit and I was tasked with ensuring it stay secure."

"So, while you were here, going after Lilith,"

"He got free," Lucifer lamented. "Before he left, however, he opened the cages, riled up the locals. There was a rebellion when my second in command launched a coup. I admit, it took longer to suppress than I'd like."

"Who's the angel?"

"We called him 'The Destroyer'. You may recognize his Hebrew name,"

"Abaddon," Gabriel chimed in, closing the door behind her as she entered.

"Sister," Lucifer greeted, unable to hide his relief. "How did you know I was here?"

"I put a tracker on you. Like the kind vets put in dogs in case they run away. I thought it was prudent after what happened last time you were in town."

"You knew what the vampire had done to me?"

"Duh," she scoffed. "I got the idea from Barachiel's wife. I thought it was pretty genius."

"*Your* idea?!"

"*You're welcome.* I knew when you came back you'd want to see that bartender chick and it would probably be helpful if she recognized you. Plus, I got used to you this way and a makeover would've just been obnoxious."

"This body was *tapped* like a *keg*."

"You weren't using it," she rebuffed. "And neither was your host. His soul had already left for Heaven, I checked. Dia was just gonna feed on those guys that attacked us and burn their bodies, but after Barachiel took off, she didn't have it in her to hunt anymore, so I set this up. Two birds."

"Why are you helping the vampires?" Valerie wondered. "I mean, I know Allydia helped us out, but they're monsters, right?"

"I've been wondering the same thing," Lucifer said.

"A," Gabriel retorted. "I made a promise to Dia back in the day that I intend on keeping. Two, she's not anywhere close to done helping us and, also, no matter how he *wishes* he felt, Barachiel has a thing for her and he would never forgive me if I let her starve herself to death."

"Not everything is your responsibility, sister."

"The hell it's not."

"I thought we were done with this demon-fighting shit," Valerie huffed.

Gabriel rolled her eyes. "You've had a three-year break. Maybe don't complain so much. Come on, Satan. Let's get you a steak, you're low on iron. Shower first, though, because *fuck*."

"Barachiel's gone?" Lucifer asked, a twinge of disappointment in his voice. "Where's he off to?"

"She won't tell me," Valerie said, folding her arms.

"Oh, a mystery. Consider my interest piqued. What's he doing that's so secretive?"

Gabriel opened the door to leave as she answered, "What he's supposed to."

Chapter 2

Wyatt stared at the ax hanging on the wall of the old barn. It seemed to stare back as if the wood and metal knew its purpose, it too not looking forward to the task at hand. Melancholy set in as he lifted it from its hook and walked back outside. He knew what he had to do, but the closer he got to the house, the more he dreaded it. As he reached his destination, he took a deep breath, raised the ax, and brought it down hard, making sure he'd only have to strike once. The wood split perfectly and he reached for another log, chopping one after another until he had a suitable amount of firewood for the night. It wasn't the physicality of the chore that he minded; it was barely work for him at all. It was just another mundane activity that *had* to be done; something else to remind him of how boring he found living out here in the middle of nothing. The past three years had been an endless, mind-numbing routine of simple but necessary tasks. The monotony of his life had become a weight around his neck, dragging him further into the depths of his depression every day. There was only one thing keeping him going. One thing that made the quiet and the banality worth it. One thing that gave him joy.

"Will," Wyatt called as he entered the farmhouse. He placed a fresh log onto the fire before heading to the kitchen. "Indiana weather," he muttered to himself. The day before, it had been sixty-two degrees. That morning, though, it had dipped back into the thirties. It was early May; his wood chopping days should have been behind him weeks ago.

The oven's timer read two minutes, so he quickly threw the salad together and pulled two sodas from the fridge. "Will, dinner!"

"I'm coming!" the boy answered, bounding down the stairs and making a beeline for the living room window.

"One second!" He pulled the curtains back just enough to peek through and watched, captivated, as the mail carrier pulled up next to the box at the end of the driveway, opened the little door, put some letters inside, and closed it back. Every evening at five on the dot, Will observed the fifty-something-year-old man deliver the mail, and every evening it brought him great happiness. He was the only person besides his father that he'd ever seen in real life, aside from his Aunt Gabriel who visited at birthdays and Christmas. Due to his condition, he wasn't allowed to leave the property or have visitors. All of his friendships were online. School, shopping, everything was done via the internet. He understood that his father was only being protective. After all, he was born three and a half years before but by every other measure was a typical sixteen-year-old. People wouldn't understand. They would bully him or worse…fear him. Will knew from watching the news that people become violent and cruel when they're afraid, even when their anxiety is unfounded. It seemed a sad truth of the human condition that people panic at the sight of something they don't fully recognize. His father was right to be worried.

"Lasagna again?" Will complained, brushing by his dad on his way to the table. Wyatt could feel a small static shock between them, but couldn't be sure of who it came from. Since Will had shown no other signs of getting his powers, he chose to ignore it.

"It's one of the few things I know how to make and can keep in the freezer for months, so yeah, lasagna again." They sat down and began to eat, Wyatt glancing at the newspaper. "Coyotes got two more dogs last night," he said after reading the front page. "You remember what to do if you see one and you're outside?"

"Keep eye contact, don't turn my back to it, and don't run."

"Good. Listen, next week I'll be doing some repairs at Pine's. I might be getting home late, so I got you some microwave dinners, just in case."

Will rolled his eyes.

"What?" Wyatt asked.

"Come on, Dad. You hate that place. I mean, I'll never complain about all the free donuts, but really. Why don't you sell it?"

"It's not that bad. I just find it tedious."

"Why do it, then? We don't need the money. We live off the money you got selling all those houses when I was a baby. There's money sitting in accounts we'll probably never need. Why do it to yourself?"

"It's not just about me, Will," Wyatt explained. "The people that work there depend on their jobs. If I sold the donut shop, a new owner would most likely cut hours, cut pay to minimum wage, get rid of their insurance. I couldn't do that to them. That's not how people should be treated. Also, it'll be a job you can do when I'm gone that won't make people too suspicious. No one does a background check on the son of the owner coming to take over the family business."

"You know what you just said, right?"

"What?"

"It's the same as always," Will said. "Everything you do is for someone else. Everything."

"Not *everything*," Wyatt assured him. "I bought that beer in the fridge just for me. Don't you even look at it sideways."

Will laughed. "Okay, Dad."

"How was school today?"

"I'm done," Will said, disappointment tingeing his voice.

"Done?"

"With high school."

"You just started."

"Like, eight months ago, Dad. I was twelve."

"My mistake," Wyatt chuckled. He didn't think he'd ever get used to how fast his son was growing. The school Will attended online was work-at-your-own-pace and his pace was rapid. Gabriel had been right about the speed of his progression and his intellect. Wyatt hoped that was all she was right about. "Well, congratulations. What do you want to do now?"

"I don't know."

"You haven't thought about it?"

"I have, it's just," He put his fork down, his face mournful. "There are some interesting degrees I could get online, but I'd have to take the SATs, so." The sadness in his voice cut Wyatt like a knife. Will was a good kid. In his entire short life, he'd never done anything worthy of punishment. He'd never once given Wyatt a reason to ground him, send him to time out, or even raise his voice. He was sweet and kind and the only thing he'd ever asked for was a faster internet connection. Wyatt couldn't bear breaking his son's heart, especially since he'd shown no signs of being dangerous. He would figure out a way.

"I'll talk to your Aunt Gabriel," Wyatt vowed. "I'm sure she knows someone who can get you some fake transcripts, social sec--"

"Really?!" Will erupted with excitement. He jumped up and hugged his father so tightly, he almost choked. "Thank you so much, Dad!" He sat back down to eat, his face beaming. He looked so much like his mother when he smiled. Wyatt now understood how his father must have felt over the years. It was heartbreaking but in the most beautiful way.

"You're thinking about Mom, aren't you?" Will asked, recognizing the pensive look on his dad's face.

"Yeah."

"Because I look like her?"

"A little, sometimes. When you're happy."

"What was she like?"

Wyatt sighed, readying himself before answering. He didn't want to be secretive about Annie the way his father had been about his own mother. He took a sip of soda and began. "She was sarcastic, like you. She was funny, sentimental, and smart. She was pretty and gentle, but strong. She was the strongest person I've ever met. She put up with a lot from me when I was sick. She saved me from myself when things were particularly bad. She was amazing."

"And she died," Will said, his tone somber. "Because of me."

"No."

"If I hadn't been bo--"

"No!" Wyatt insisted. Will had never seen his father look so stern. It was unnerving. "Your mother had a massive stroke that caused irreparable brain damage. It was *biology*. It was not your fault, do you hear me?"

Will nodded.

"I really want you to get this. You have zero blame in what happened to your mother. None."

"Okay," Will accepted. They went back to eating their dinner in silence for a while until Will spoke again, thinking it necessary to point something out. "Dad," he said, his voice quiet.

"Yeah?"

"It wasn't your fault either."

Wyatt looked up at his son, his features softening. He knew he needed to set a good example, to show Will that he didn't have to be burdened with guilt over things he had no control over, so he lied. "I know that."

A few days later, it was finally happening. His aunt had come through with the paperwork and gotten Will signed up to take the test. He was giddy, riding in the car for the first time, his father also smiling as they drove into town. Wyatt had never seen Will so happy, the spring wind blowing through the open window, gently tousling the boy's dark hair. They pulled into the high school's parking lot and found a spot.

"You have everything you need?" Wyatt asked.

"Yeah," Will answered, anxious to get inside.

"Okay, I'll be right here when you're done. Remember, it's not life and death, it's just a test. Have some fun."

"Thanks, Dad. I'll try." Will opened the car door and got out. He slammed it shut, not meaning to close it so hard, and waved goodbye, hurrying toward the entrance. Wyatt felt an immense sense of pride as he waved back, his anxiety about Will's first outing fading.

"He's a good kid," he reminded himself. "He'll be fine." As Will disappeared behind the double doors, Wyatt's phone rang. He glanced at the number. It was the shop. "This is Wyatt," he answered.

"Hey, it's Charlie," the woman on the other end said. "Can you come by? The girls aren't doing very well."

"What's wrong?"

She was quiet for a moment. "You haven't heard?"

"Apparently not."

"Can you just come by? I should really tell you in person."

"On my way." He ended the call and started the car. The SATs would take hours. He'd be back in plenty of time.

Inside, Will waited on pins and needles for the test to begin. The air was thick with the nervous energy of other kids, squirming in their seats, the cold cafeteria providing little comfort in its sterility. He tried to focus on the instructor at the head of the room, not wanting to miss anything important, but his attention was quickly diverted by a girl pulling up a chair next to him.

"Hi," she said brightly. She was gorgeous and smelled like birthday cake, one tawny shoulder peeking from the collar of her pink top. The fluorescent light bounced off her curls like starlight and the stare from her honey eyes made his stomach jump.

"Hi," he said shakily.

"I'm Michelle," she said. "First time?"

"How'd you know?"

"Most people only take the SATs once. This is my second time. I just wanted to see if I could get a better score."

"Oh," he said, relieved that she had been referring to the test and couldn't tell from his awkward behavior that this was the first time he'd ever spoken to a girl. "Do you go here? I mean, you look--"

"Old?" she giggled. "I'm twenty-one, so, no, I don't go here. I still haven't gone to college, though. I got into a bunch of schools, I just don't know if it's for me. What about you? College plans?"

"A few. I'm interested in Culinary Arts and History, but I'll probably get a Business degree first, just to be prepared."

"Sounds ambitious." She looked toward the front of the room where the instructor had begun passing out booklets. "Looks like we're starting." She got up and snuck back to her original seat and whispered, "Good luck."

"You, too." He readied his pencil, stunned that an impossibly beautiful girl had spoken to him out of the blue. If this was what being out in the world was like, he could very well become addicted. *Calm down*, he thought, the booklet sliding on the table in front of him. *Time to focus.*

Wyatt entered the donut shop to find the place nearly deserted, unusual for this early in the morning. Charlie, the shop's manager, rushed to greet him while Marley and Rose stood behind the counter, both barely keeping it together, the younger woman's cheeks stained with smeared mascara while Rose still wiped away tears of her own.

"What's going on?" Wyatt asked.

"It's Tim," Charlie explained. "He didn't show up to work this morning, so I called him, but no answer. The sheriff came in about an hour ago and told us," She paused for a moment to collect herself. "He said Tim's dead."

"Oh, my God," he said. Tim was the head baker at Pine's and everyone in town loved him. He was a veteran of the Iraq War and had received a Purple Heart after saving a convoy, taking an IED blast that eventually got him fitted with a titanium leg. Despite the severe spinal nerve pain he lived with every day, he always seemed to be in a good mood, putting a smile on the faces of everyone he came across. He was the closest thing Wyatt had to a friend in this town. He would be missed. "How?"

"They found him in the creek by the park. The sheriff said it looked like a coyote attack. He's asking the mayor to let people hunt them. He thinks there's at least one that's gone rabid."

"Okay," he said, placing a comforting hand on the older woman's shoulder. "You should all go home. I'll close up."

"Are you sure?" Rose called from the counter, finally getting her emotions under control.

"Yeah, go ahead. I'll pay you for eight hours. Take the day, get some rest. Customers will understand. Marley, I'm promoting you to head baker. Can you start tomorrow? Take over Tim's hours?"

She was flattered. "Really?"

"You know the job, you've filled in before. I can find another cashier, but teaching someone new to make the donuts like Tim did?" He shook his head. "You're the only one."

"But, Rose has seniority."

Rose laughed. "Dear, I'm retiring in a month. No way I'm taking on more responsibility."

"You can do this, Marley," Charlie assured her.

The twenty-year-old couldn't believe it. This was her dream job, having grown up eating there every Saturday since she was a baby. She felt guilty for being happy in that moment, but couldn't help but smile. "Thank you, Mr. Sinclair."

"Wyatt," he insisted. "You guys get out of here. Take some donuts with you. I'll see you tomorrow."

The ladies collected their belongings, each taking a dozen donuts as they headed out. Wyatt cashed out the drawers and put a help-wanted sign in the window before filling several boxes with the remaining donuts and leaving himself, locking the door behind him. He got in his car and sat, the gravity of Tim's death hitting him like a ton of bricks. While he felt the loss wholly, he knew there was someone else taking it much harder. He leaned back in his seat and closed his eyes for a moment before whispering to himself, "Shit."

Wyatt knocked on the door of Tim's house to no answer. His wife, Sydney, was either not home or couldn't bring herself to come to the door. As he was about to leave, he noticed the letter carrier stopping at the mailbox.

"Hey, Arthur," he called as he approached.

"Wyatt," the man said gloomily. "Sorry to hear."

"Yeah, listen, I know it's not technically allowed, but Sydney's not home and I'd like to leave her something. Could I maybe sneak it in the mailbox?"

"Well, that's against Federal law," Arthur reminded him. "But, I can't report what I don't see."

"Understood."

"Such a shame about that boy. At least he didn't leave any kids behind. His poor wife, though."

Wyatt nodded in agreement.

"Well, I better get back to it. Not rain, nor sleet nor dead war heroes."

"I'll see you later, Arthur."

"See you later."

Wyatt waited for the mail truck to turn the corner before placing the envelope in the letterbox. The thirty-five thousand dollar check inside would do little to alleviate the despair he knew Tim's widow must be feeling, but a year's wages was all he could think to offer. She shouldn't have to worry about paying her bills on top of everything else. He knew what it was like to lose someone and Tim was such an important part of Pine's and the community, it was the least he could do.

"How was it?" Wyatt asked as Will got in the car.

"Awesome!" Will gushed, smiling from ear to ear. "I was nervous being around all those people, but it was *so* worth it. When can I go out again?"

"We'll see."

"You don't understand. It was amazing. Dad, a *girl* talked to me."

"A girl?" Wyatt chuckled as he drove from the parking lot to the street. "I've given you 'the talk', right?"

"Yeah, Dad," Will sighed, rolling his eyes. "A bunch of times."

Wyatt laughed again. "Okay, as long as you remember the three golden rules."

"Respect, consent, and condoms."

"Good boy," Wyatt snickered. "Seriously, though, I'm really proud of you. Finishing school, being around people. You're doing well. You're a great kid."

"Um, thanks."

"You know you're the best part of my life, right?"

"I know."

"I love you like crazy. And your mom loved you, too. More than anything."

"Why are you being weird?"

Wyatt sighed. "Something happened today that reminded me how important it is to let the people you love know how much they mean to you. I don't want you to ever not know how loved you are."

"Okay, Dad. I love you, too," Will said, patting his father on the arm. "Now, let me tell you about this girl."

Chapter 3

The eerie glow of the computer screen lit up Lucifer's face as he searched the internet for news of outbreaks and for a moment, Gabriel got a glimpse of how the Fallen must see him in Hell; cold, focused, and creepy as shit. She got a bottle of water from the fridge and set it next to him on the bar.

"Thank you, Gabriel," he said, unscrewing the cap. "I was getting quite parched."

"I know," she said, shoving her phone in her back pocket and rifling through kitchen drawers. "Have you seen my checkbook?"

"You still use one of those? I thought they went extinct, like black and white televisions or common courtesy."

"Believe it or not, if you look hard enough, you can still find those things."

"I'll take your word for it. I may have seen it in the pantry this morning when I was attempting to locate something edible. I failed miserably, by the way."

"You didn't eat?" she asked, finding what she was looking for and setting it on the counter. *Five million dollars*, she scribbled in the amount section.

"Everything calling itself 'food' in this apartment is either full of chemicals or dripping with sugar, mostly both. I ordered in. Someone will be delivering it shortly. I took the liberty of purchasing you something, as well."

"Thank you, Lucifer, that's very kind. Save it for me, will you? I have to run an errand. I shouldn't be more than an hour." She finished filling out the check and tore it from the book. As she headed toward the door, she called back to her brother, "Try not to kill anyone while I'm gone."

He waved, not looking up from the screen in front of him. "Demons running amok," he muttered to himself, unhappy with how long this was taking. Nearly a week had passed since he'd been back and he still had nothing to show for it. His impatience grew like weeds, fertilized by guilt. "I will set things right, Father. I swear it."

Gabriel walked into the small Chinatown shop, her boots clicking on the tile as she passed towering displays of colorful, unrelated items. Handbags on a rack with bathing suits hung next to a table of cleaning supplies and baby-proofing devices. As she approached the counter, the old woman behind it barked, "Ni xiang yao shenme?!"

"She says, 'How can we help you?'" her grandson told Gabriel, who knew that wasn't *exactly* what she'd said.

"There's an amulet in a silver-lined black box on the top shelf of your storage room, closest to the office. I need it," Gabriel answered plainly, taking the check from her pocket.

The older woman recoiled, having gone from suspicious to horrified. She yelled at the teenager in Mandarin, ordering him to make the stranger leave. Gabriel's exasperation was evident to the boy, the shop owner's panic-induced word vomit bordering on insulting.

"Oh, Christ, I'm not a witch," she rebuffed. The woman silenced herself, surprised that the stranger understood. The two watched as she unfolded the check and slid it across to them. "I know you've been getting a lot of shit from your asshole landlord," Gabriel explained. "He's raising the rent and being an all-around dick because he wants to sell the building. This is enough to buy it yourself and tell him to fuck off."

They examined the check, their jaws dropping.

"I need that item," she demanded. The boy rushed to the back to retrieve it while his grandmother wrung her hands.

"It's okay," he whispered to the old woman as he handed the box to Gabriel. "She doesn't know how to use it."

As she left, Gabriel turned back. "I know exactly what I'll have to do with it."

Gabriel closed the door behind her after entering the apartment to find a note on top of a takeout container next to the still-open laptop.

Measles outbreak in the Philippines. Will check in if any news.

"This motherfucker," she murmured. She hid the box in the back of the pantry and sat at the bar, opening the container to find an egg white omelet. She took a bite and gagged as she swallowed. "Spinach," she choked, covering her mouth. "At least it's not cold." She took another bite, wincing as she chewed. She logged onto a crowdfunding site and searched for medical fundraisers. She lazily clicked, fully funding several of them as she ate.

I'm bored. Come over, she thought.

I'm at work, Valerie responded.

Quit your job. I'll give you ten million dollars right now.

You know I'm not doing that.

You're dumb.

Bitch, bye.

Fine. She took a sip from Lucifer's half-empty water bottle before contacting another sibling. *Hey, B.*

Hi, Gabriel, Wyatt replied.

How's Will? Murdery yet?

He's fine, he thought with derision.

Good, that's good. How are you? You need anything? Money? A babysitter? Five minutes back in civilization just to remember what it feels like?

I'm all right. What about you? You sound--

Bored?

Lonely.

Gabriel raised her eyebrows in silent agreement before noticing the time. *I have an appointment. Talk to you later. Keep an eye on that kid.*

I always do.

"We need to talk about your spending," he said, his voice stern. Gabriel sat across from the accountant who stared at her, clearly displeased. The office was stark and flooded with light coming in from the windows behind the middle-aged, balding man who sat straight up in his chair, not an ounce of calm in his demeanor. She tried to focus on the view, but couldn't get the image of him and his cleaning lady out of her head. The two had had a tryst the night before on this very desk and since he was still thinking about it, she too was stuck with the mental impression.

"Okay," she dismissed.

"It's reckless."

"Reckless," she scoffed.

"Ms. Murphy,"

"You're getting bent out of shape over charitable donations."

"You're giving away *sixty percent* of your money."

"Sixty percent of three billion dollars still leaves me with stupid amounts of money to blow on takeout and candy."

"You're being glib."

"I'm being honest. Listen, I know you want me to invest in stocks, buy rental property, create my own foundation as a tax haven; all that normal rich person bullshit. But, I'm not going to. To be honest, I plan on giving *more* money away. There are a lot of people that need it way more than I do."

The accountant sighed and rubbed his brow, looking fondly at his client who he'd been working with for the past two decades. "I'll be straight with you," he said, folding his hands and leaning across the desk. "I admire that you want to help people, I do, but I wouldn't be doing my job if I didn't warn you against what you're doing. If you keep spending at this rate while leaving your automatic monthly donations in place, you'll run out of money in less than a hundred years."

"I'm relatively certain I'll be dead by then, bro."

"Don't you want to leave something for your children?"

Gabriel laughed. "I'm *definitely* not having those."

"Oh."

"I understand your concern. You're just doing your job, and you're good at it, really. But, using my parents' money to help people that need it is like my silver lining. I *have* to do it."

"I see. It makes their deaths seem like they weren't in vain."

"No, it makes their lives seem like they were worth something. Those people were trash."

"Oh, uh, um,"

"We done?" Gabriel asked, standing to leave.

"I suppose."

"Awesome. See you next month."

Gabriel stood in the mausoleum, not really sure what she was doing there. She almost never thought about her parents anymore, since doing so only made her angry and she had enough to worry about without being distracted by emotions that no longer mattered. She folded her arms and looked over the plaques.

James R. Murphy 1948-1997

Esther M. Murphy 1953-1997

Beloved parents

"Bullshit," she whispered to herself. She glared at the stone wall for a few more seconds, the rage bubbling over. She didn't like how she felt and she hated more that she was wasting her time and energy on criminals that should have been long forgotten. Before she turned to leave, she took a step closer to the tombs. She knew they couldn't hear her, their souls firmly in Purgatory, but she had to say it anyway. "Fuck you."

Chapter 4

"Last one," Wyatt said to himself, twisting the light bulb into place. "Fixed," he sighed, proud of the job he'd done repairing the sign. He'd been told that it was a lost cause, that the decades-old sign should be replaced, but he knew what the shop meant to the people of Southport. It was a landmark to them, part of the town's history. He was still a relative newcomer and if he started making big changes, it may not sit too well with some of the residents. The last thing he wanted to do was bring negative attention to himself.

As he made his way down the rickety ladder, he heard the sound of glass breaking. It was late, well after most people on the quiet street were typically out and about. He walked around the building, following the noise to the dumpster in the back. At first, he thought it was the rabid coyote that had been terrorizing the town, but the dumpster shook, scooting a little on the concrete underneath. Something was inside and it was way bigger than a coyote. *Teenagers*, he thought.

"Hey!" Wyatt called. No answer. It occurred to him that the person inside might be homeless, hungry, and looking for food. "Hey, if you're hungry, I have a few donuts left from this morning! You're welcome to them!" The shaking stopped. "I'll go put those in a bag for you! Meet you out front!" He turned to enter the building through the service door, but before he could get the key from his pocket, he heard a low, guttural growl.

"Oh, shit," he whispered. Wyatt had been warned about the woods behind the donut shop, that on a rare occasion, a black bear might wander through. He'd never seen one there, but he now gathered the electricity from the air and formed a ball of lightning, ready to face the beast. He spun around, ready to fire, but he was so taken aback by what he saw that the electricity gathered in his hand dissipated, curiosity and confusion clouding his judgement. What stood on the lid of the dumpster in front of him was a man, only not. He was naked, covered from head to toe in long, dark hair with flecks of gray about the face. His arms seemed stretched and spider-like with black claws erupting from four gnarled fingers on each oversized hand. His legs were bent backward, the way a dog's would be. Large, pointed ears sprung up from his malformed head above eyes that shone in the dark like a cat's.

Gabriel, Wyatt thought.

Yeah, B? she replied.

Quick question. Are werewolves real?

Eh, kind of. There used to be a few Native American tribes that could shapeshift into wolves for hunting purposes, but the Colonists killed most of them off in the seventeenth century. There have been a handful of times when a half-person/half-wolf monster movie type of thing would pop up, but there hasn't been one of those for like, two hundred years or so. Why?

Because I'm either hallucinating or I'm looking at one right now. He told his sister, watching the creature slowly climb down.

For real?! Light that thing's ass up! It will rip your throat out before you can say 'lycanthropy'. You're not on drugs, right? No brown acid?

Stone-cold sober.

Well, damn, dude, get to smiting. Pew pew!

The beast growled again, bearing his long, pointed teeth. He moved carefully, examining his prey. In an instant, he pounced, leaping forward with unnatural speed. Wyatt threw a bolt of lightning into the monster's chest, sending it falling back and yelping in pain. He darted on all fours into the woods just as the sign in front sparked and went out.

"Fuck me," Wyatt muttered.

You okay? Gabriel asked.

Yeah, but it got away. I'm going after it.

Not what I would recommend, but you do you, fam.

Wyatt entered the woods, the lush greenery blocking out all light from the street. He searched for several minutes, the moon his only guide. There were no signs of the creature. Wyatt was about to give up when he heard a branch snap. He went in the direction of the noise but was stopped in his tracks by a middle-aged woman with gray hair and almond-shaped eyes.

"You need to leave," she commanded.

"You shouldn't be out here right now, ma'am," he told her.

"I'm aware of the creature. My people have ways of dealing with things like this, but you are not safe. Go, before it returns. Here," She handed him a business card. "If you see it again, call my brother. *We* will handle it."

She walked off into the dark, leaving Wyatt feeling frustrated and useless. He hated the idea of that thing still out there, hurting people. It had killed his friend. Who would be next? He looked down at the card. *Mills Auto Sales.* He let out a defeated sigh and put the card in his pocket, trekking back to the shop. After taking the electricity from the sign to fight off the werewolf, it was, again, in need of repairs.

Michelle sat at the small table in the donut shop, going over her application for the second time, making sure she'd filled everything out properly. She was pleasantly surprised to see no box for race, assuming it meant that the management wasn't overly concerned with a potential employee's ethnicity. She took a bite of the free donut the manager had given her while she waited, glancing around the room, taking note of where the exits were and what everyday items could be used as weapons in an emergency. The building was old, but clean and had a hominess about it that reminded her of her grandparents' house. They had died when she was small, but she could still remember making dorayaki with her baa-baa every Saturday in her small, upstate kitchen. The donuts here were good, but they couldn't compare.

"You all done?" Charlie asked. Michelle nodded and the older woman sat across from her, taking the application and giving it a quick once-over. "So, you used to be a personal assistant?"

"Yes, ma'am."

"You can just call me Charlie. We're not sticklers for formality around here," the manager said, a friendly smile crossing her unpainted lips. "What were your job duties?"

"Answering the phone, making appointments, running errands. Anything my boss didn't want to deal with herself. Most of the time, it was just a lot of store runs for chocolate."

Charlie laughed before moving on. "In 'special skills' you wrote, 'Krav Maga' and 'Brazilian Jiu Jitsu'."

"I also type fifty-five words a minute."

Charlie laughed again. "I like you. Can you start tomorrow? Five-thirty AM on the dot. Starting pay is twelve dollars an hour. That goes up to fifteen after thirty days which is also when your insurance kicks in."

"I get insurance? But, I'd only be part-time."

"The owner's a nice guy. Not like the last one, who was a real hard-ass. Don't tell Mr. Sinclair I said that, though. He was his uncle. When Wyatt took over about three years ago, he raised everyone's pay, got us better insurance, upgraded our equipment. He's the best boss I've ever had. You'll like him."

"He sounds like an angel," Michelle said, struggling not to laugh.

"He's been one for us."

"I will definitely see you tomorrow," Michelle told her, standing to leave, taking what remained of her donut with her.

"See you then!"

The two shook hands and Michelle left the building, popping the donut in her mouth before taking her phone from her pocket and texting, *Job secured.*

Chapter 5

Valerie woke up shivering, her blanket having been stolen by the handsome man sleeping next to her. Sunlight filled the room, causing her to squint while she sleepily looked at the time. "Oh, fuck!" she blurted, jumping out of bed and racing around the room, picking up pieces of clothing as she went.

"What's up?" Malik asked, rubbing his eyes as he sat up.

"What's up is I'm three hours late," Valerie griped. "My alarm didn't go off. Help me find my bra."

Malik grinned as he pulled the garment from under his pillow and twirled it in the air. "You're not late. Come back to bed."

"Boy, you see what time it is? Quit playin'."

"Your alarm went off. I called the school and told them you were sick so we could spend the day together."

She tilted her head and looked him over. "I don't know if that's cute or intrusive, but you lookin' sexy as hell, so I guess I'm okay with it." She giggled as she hopped back in bed, taking the bra from him and throwing it to the floor. She climbed on top of him and started to kiss him, but he protested.

"Hold up," he said, opening and reaching into the nightstand's drawer. He took out a small box and opened it to reveal a white gold and diamond engagement ring. "Valerie Moore,"

"Yes!" she squealed.

"You gonna let me ask?"

"Nuh, uh!" she said, taking the ring and putting it on her own finger. "I don't wanna give you a chance to change your mind."

He laughed. "I would never."

"You better not."

Lucifer sat pensively, the computer screen mocking him with its aggressively bright light and lack of useful information. Every lead so far had turned out to be an utter waste of time. The world had become a cesspool of disease, famine, war, and poverty. It was impossible to distinguish demonic activity, Abaddon's handiwork, and humanity's own self-destruction. He was beyond frustrated and needed to kill something.

"Cheer up, Satan," Gabriel poked. "At least you got a little color while you were out chasing the big bad."

"I do wish you'd stop calling me that," he sighed. "Satan is a myth, a figment of mankind's imagination, used to scapegoat their own less socially acceptable behaviors. I, as you can see, very much exist."

"Yes, you do. Speaking of things that exist, a little birdie told me there's a demon nest in the Atlantic Avenue Tunnel. I was thinking we could check it out, exorcise some bitches then hit the speakeasy." She did a little dance while Lucifer moaned in annoyance.

"These demons," he complained. "Every time I send five back to their cages, ten more appear in their place. Like gray hairs or Hydra."

"Shh," she instructed, waving for him to be quiet. She looked to the front door, then back to him. "Be nice." She opened the door before Valerie could knock, which Valerie usually found irritating. Today, though, she was too happy to notice, excited to share her news with her sister. She held her hand up to show off her new ring, her smile infectious.

"Congrats, lady," Gabriel said, taking Valerie's hand to look at the ring more closely.

"You're getting married, Uriel?" Lucifer questioned. "Is that wise?"

"What did I tell you?" Gabriel scolded.

"I'm only curious as to how our dear sister will keep her true identity from her beloved. Tell me, is he a religious man?"

"Uh-uh," she dismissed. "Not today, Satan. You are not getting to me *today*. I came here to celebrate with my girl."

"Yas, bitch," Gabriel agreed. The women broke out into an impromptu dance-off, further worsening Lucifer's vexation.

"I will handle the nest alone," he decided, standing from the barstool and leaving the apartment.

"Don't let the door hit ya!" Valerie called, still dancing.

"I have to do it," Gabriel said, pulling up a video on her phone.

"Don't you do it," Valerie joked. "Don't do it!"

"I'm doing it!"

As the song began to play, their dancing became more coordinated.

"Girl," Valerie said. "You know I have to shake it to a song named for me."

"You wouldn't happen to know where Abaddon is, would you?" Lucifer asked the demon he'd beaten nearly to death. He'd made quick work of exorcising the rest of the nest and he was sure this one would have no answers for him, but he had to make the attempt.

"Abaddon?" the demon laughed, blood pouring from his nose and mouth. "You should be focusing your efforts on more pressing matters, Watch Keeper. Abaddon is but one, while we are Legion. There are thousands of us on Father's precious planet. How angry do you think He'll be with you when He finds out you let us roam free in order to chase one rogue angel?"

Lucifer seethed, fully aware of the consequences of his prolonged search. He punched the demon several more times, even after the vermin had lost consciousness, trying to release the discontent he felt. He then placed his hand on the man's chest, watching with delight as the shadowy figure left the body and went screaming back to its cage.

Lucifer brushed his hands together, glaring at the bodies around him before opining, "This is taking too long."

"Next weekend, Atlantic City, family and close friends only," Valerie said.

"You know I'll be there," Gabriel told her.

"And invite Wyatt. I haven't seen that boy in forever. There's no excuse good enough for missing your sister's wedding."

"I don't know if that's a good idea. He's pretty busy."

"Bitch, I couldn't give less of a fuck if I was born without reproductive organs. You make sure he gets his ass there."

"Okay," Gabriel chuckled. "It's your day. I will make it happen."

"Good."

"What about Lucifer?"

"Ugh, do I have to?"

"Uriel,"

"Fine, but he better be on his best behavior. I can't have him embarrassing me in front of Malik's parents. Those people barely tolerate me as it is."

"I promise to throw him out a window if he acts up."

"That's all I ask. I'm gonna go. Mrs. Perry wants to take me dress shopping. Wish me luck. I'm gonna need it." As Valerie closed the door behind her, Gabriel's phone rang.

"Hey, Hattie," she answered. The girl on the other end was distraught, barely able to form words. Too impatient to tell her to calm herself and slow down, Gabriel instead simply said, "On my way."

Gabriel peeked into Allydia's room, what she saw there giving her a better understanding of Hattie's panic. The vampire was ghostly pale, her hair dull and unwashed, eyes distant, lying on top of the sheets, her face gaunt.

"It's worse than before," Hattie said quietly, coming to stand next to Gabriel in the hall. "She's not only refusing to hunt or feed, she won't even take blood from a glass. At least before, she was drinking *something*. Now, she desiccates. She will die if she continues this way. I'm at a loss. I've never seen her like this."

"I have," Gabriel said. "A long time ago." She stood there for a few seconds, watching Allydia's stillness, a twinge of guilt gnawing at the back of her mind. She had done the right thing in sending Wyatt away. Still, Allydia's reaction was more dramatic than she'd anticipated. She genuinely felt sorry for her and hoped she'd be able to pull herself out of this depression faster than she had the last time. "If she's still not eating in two days, call me back. I'll hold her down so you can feeding tube the drama queen. Even in her weakened state, she's stronger than any of you." She walked to the door and looked back at Hattie who was feeling relieved and grateful for Gabriel's assistance. "She just needs time."

Chapter 6

Wyatt placed his hand over the coals of the grill. *Not hot enough*, he thought. He took a deep breath, the fresh, "green" scent of a just-mowed lawn hanging in the finally-warm air. One of the few things he enjoyed about living out here was how picturesque it was when spring hit. Everything was flowering and full of life. The landscape was so beautiful, he forgot for a moment about the creature that had attacked him two nights before. But, as his eyes lifted to the woods beyond the barn, he couldn't help but remember, hoping that the strange woman he'd met that night had taken care of it.

"You finally gonna let me wield the spatula?" Will teased, bringing the steaks out from the kitchen.

"You know what? I think I will," Wyatt agreed.

"Seriously?"

"Sure, you're in college now. I think you can handle it."

"Thanks, Dad!"

"Grill's not ready yet, though. Give it a few minutes."

Will nodded and put the plate down on the picnic table a few feet away, his eyes glued to the low flames stirring under the coals. "Oh, crap!" he shouted. "What time is it?"

Wyatt checked his phone. "Five o two."

"CRAP!" Will darted back into the house and headed for the front window. He was sure he'd missed Arthur delivering the day's mail, but to his delight, the carrier was still there, setting letters in the box. "Whew," Will breathed. He watched the man walk back to his truck, but instead of getting inside as Will expected, he gathered a package from behind the seat and began the long walk to the front porch. "Oh, jeez," Will mumbled, leaping from the couch and running through the house to the backyard. "Dad!" he called.

"What's going on?" Wyatt asked.

"The mailman's coming to the door."

"Okay, I'll get it. You know what to do."

He did. It had only happened a few times over the years, but there was a routine in place for when someone unexpectedly dropped by. Will would stay in the kitchen while his father got rid of whoever was at the door. There would be no way to explain who he was to people without coming up with an elaborate story that wouldn't hold water a few months later when he'd have grown another two years. It was safer for him to avoid being seen as much as possible until he was an adult and the aging process normalized.

The carrier knocked just as Will stood behind the wall that separated the kitchen from the living room. He gave his father a thumbs up from the entrance and Wyatt opened the door.

"Hey, Arthur," he said cheerfully. "You need me to sign for that?"

"Yeah," the man stated, handing Wyatt a pen. "It's marked 'signature required'. Must be important." Wyatt glanced at the return address on the box. It was from his father. He scribbled his name and returned the pen.

"Hey, is that one of those 4K TVs?" Arthur asked, pointing to the entertainment center.

"Yeah," Wyatt confirmed. "A gift from my sister."

"I've been thinkin' about gettin' me one of those. I've had the same old plasma screen since 'Monk' ended." He stepped forward to have a better look, poking his head in the doorway and bumping into Wyatt. "Ope."

"You're fine," Wyatt told him, but as the man stepped back, his face changed. He looked distant, then aggravated. "You okay, Arthur?" Wyatt asked, worried the older man was having a stroke. Arthur put his hand on his chest and moved closer, placing a hand on Wyatt's shoulder. "I'm calling an ambulance," Wyatt said, taking his phone from his pocket, but before he could dial the number, he noticed the man's skin slowly covering itself in a thin layer of hair. Arthur sniffed the air, then Wyatt. His eyes grew wider and began to change shape, becoming rounder with longer lashes as he stared angrily into the eyes of the man he now knew had hurt him two nights before. His teeth lengthened, cutting his bottom lip, and as he gripped Wyatt's shoulder, he let out a low, quiet growl.

"Holy shit," Wyatt whispered. Without hesitation, he shoved the man off the porch, slamming the door shut and locking the deadbolt and chain. He ran to the kitchen and took the business card from the junk drawer, handing it along with his phone to his son. "Call this number," he instructed. "Tell them 'it's here' and give them our address." Loud banging came from the door, violently shaking it and startling Will. "Go to the basement. Lock the door. Don't come out until I tell you. Now!" He pushed Will in the direction of the basement door just a few feet away. The boy complied, moving as quickly as he could. He dialed the number on the card and waited impatiently for someone to pick up.

"Mills Auto Sales," the man on the other end said. "We've got what you're looking for. How can I help you?"

"Hi, um, I'm supposed to tell you, 'it's here'."

The man was quiet for a second before responding, his tone changed. "Where are you?"

Will gave him the address and the man ended the call without another word. Will pressed his ear to the door, hearing a crash and the sound of glass breaking. "Arthur!" he could hear his father yell. "Snap out of it! Remember who you are!"

But he couldn't. The wolf had taken over. He lunged for Wyatt, who held him off with small, low energy lightning blasts. "I don't want to hurt you!" Wyatt shouted. The wolfman kept coming, all but ignoring the shocks, seeming to develop an immunity.

Will felt afraid, wanting to help his father, but not knowing how. He did the only thing he could think of. He called his Aunt Gabriel.

"Hello?" she answered.

"Aunt Gabriel, it's me, Will."

"Hey, sweetie. What's up?"

"I don't even know. Dad's fighting with the mailman or something. It's really loud. I'm in the basement, but--"

"But nothing," she said sternly. "You stay your ass there until your dad comes to get you, do you hear me? He can handle himself, trust me."

"That's what he told me to do, but what if--"

"Stay. There."

"But--"

"Boy,"

"Okay, okay." He heard another crash, this one so violent, it shook the lightbulb that hung overhead. "I have to go."

"Will--" Gabriel protested as he hit the 'end call' button. He again pressed his ear to the door to try to hear what was happening on the other side.

"Arthur, stop!" Wyatt shouted, throwing a low voltage bolt into the creature's chest. He was as he had been behind Pine's, tall, animal-like and crazed. He swung his elongated arm, knocking Wyatt to the floor. He grasped him by the throat with one giant, clawed hand and slammed him down through the coffee table. Wyatt grabbed the beast's arm and shocked him again, this time with more force. The wolfman winced but did not relent. He held Wyatt there, choking the life from him.

Will could hear his father's gasps for air and the odd growling of an animal he didn't recognize. His heart pounded in his chest as he put his hand to the doorknob. His dad was dying. He was *dying*. He had to do something, so he opened the basement door and raced to the living room where he was stunned by what stood before him. It was like something out of a comic; a monster, enormous and looming, hovering over his father, one gigantic hand around his neck, the other in the air, ready to strike. Wyatt's face was purple, his eyes bulging. Spurts of blue light erupted from his hands every few seconds, which seemed to hurt the animal, but not enough to stop it. Adrenaline surged through Will's veins as panic set in. His heart was beating so loudly in his ears that he could no longer hear the creature's growls. Wyatt's head tilted back and for a second, he and Will locked eyes.

"Run," he gurgled, but Will shook his head. Instead, he rushed forward, throwing himself, full speed into the monster. When he made contact, a hot, white light poured from his hands like water through a busted dam. The power of it was so strong that it knocked the boy back and to the ground. The light flew into the wolf, causing it to convulse and foam at the mouth. It fell back, its eyes bursting in its head and smoke rising from its singed fur.

Wyatt coughed, putting his hand to his throat and taking slow, labored breaths, rolling over and eventually standing himself up. Will, too, stood, looking at the dead creature and down at his hands. "What did I do?" he whispered.

"It's okay," Wyatt said.

"It's not okay! What did I do, Dad?!"

Wyatt hugged his son tightly, grabbing the back of his neck and kissing his head. "It's okay," he repeated.

"What did I do?" the boy said again, tears streaming down his face.

"You saved me," Wyatt told him, tears now in his eyes, as well. "You saved us both."

"I didn't mean to hurt him," Will sobbed into his father's shoulder. "I didn't mean to, to--"

"I know."

"I just wanted to get him off you," the boy wept. "I didn't want to--"

"I know. Listen," Wyatt said, releasing his embrace and taking Will's face in his hands. "Arthur was a good guy, but that thing wasn't Arthur. It was a monster that took him over. It killed Tim and it would have killed us and who knows how many more people if you hadn't stopped it. I know it hurts, believe me. I've felt the guilt you're feeling, but you saved lives putting that thing down. I wish you didn't have to. I wish there was something I could've done to save Arthur, but there wasn't. Arthur was gone. Do you understand?"

Will nodded, wiping the tears from his cheeks.

"Hello," a man said, walking into the house through the opening where the front door used to be. He stood over the corpse, a puzzled look coming over his face. "How did you do this?"

"We electrocuted it," Wyatt said.

"With what, the power grid?"

"How did this happen? I was told werewolves haven't existed for centuries."

"He was out hunting a few weeks back," the man explained. "He came across one of us and her cub. He thought they were normal gray wolves, got nervous, raised his gun. The baby got scared and bit him, just trying to protect his mother. He's only four years old. He didn't know what he was doing."

"Would he have ever gone back to normal?" Will wondered.

"No," the forty-something-year-old man answered, sweeping his long hair off his shoulder. "Once the wolf has you, there is no going back. The man would have slipped away over time, losing all memory of his former self. His humanity would be lost. All there would be for him was the kill."

"That's enough, Joseph," the woman from the woods said as she entered with another man. "You two, take the body to the truck. I'll finish up here."

The men wrapped the creature in a blue tarp and lifted him up, struggling under the weight as they carried the wolfman out of the house.

"I assume I don't have to tell you that this can't get out," she said.

"No shit."

"Will," Wyatt scolded, never having heard him use that language before.

"Sorry."

"Good," the woman said, glaring at Will and back at Wyatt. "I need to speak to you. Alone."

Wyatt motioned for Will to go upstairs and he did, no questions asked.

"What happened here?" she asked. Wyatt gave her a look of refusal and shook his head. "Fine," she said, looking up the stairs. "We're all entitled to our secrets, but I have a bad feeling about him. I don't know what that boy is, but you keep him on a tight leash." She stormed out, again leaving Wyatt with more questions than answers.

Yo, B, you okay? he heard in his head.

I'm fine, he responded. *Werewolf's dead. Locals came and picked it up.*

Cool. How's Will? He was pretty shaken up when he called.

He's okay. I have some cleaning to do. I'll talk to you later.

K.

Wyatt looked up to see his son creeping down the stairs. "I saw their truck leave from my window," he said.

"Are you all right?"

"Not really."

"I'm sorry. Listen, Will, we need to have a talk. There are things you don't know. Who we are, what we can do."

"At the risk of getting snapped at again, no shit."

"Will,"

"You've been lying to me. I don't just have some super rare aging disorder, do I?"

"No. I didn't tell you because I was hoping you wouldn't inherit my--"

"Can we talk about it after dinner, Dad? The grill's gotta be hot by now and I'm starving."

"So, what are we, Dad?" Will asked, dropping his fork and folding his arms. "Aliens? We're aliens, right? Is there a ship buried under the barn? Are we waiting for someone to beam us up and fly us to our home planet? Is Gabriel really your sister, or is she a government spook assigned to make sure we don't blow up the planet with our advanced technology?"

"I don't appreciate your attitude," Wyatt said, finishing his last bite of steak.

"I don't appreciate being lied to."

"Fair enough." He took a sip of beer while he tried to put the words together. He'd dreaded this conversation, hoping they'd never have to have it. He put the bottle down and reluctantly began, deciding that the only way to explain it was to just spit it out. "My body is human. I was born like everyone else. I have parents, I grew up on West 72nd Street in Manhattan, went to school, had friends. All the things I told you about my life are true. But, a few years ago, Gabriel came to me and told me who I was inside. Basically, instead of a soul, I have...I'm an angel."

Will chuckled, thinking his father was pulling his leg in an attempt to lighten the mood. But Wyatt's face remained still. He wasn't kidding.

"Really?" Will asked. "An angel?"

"Guardian angel, specifically. Barachiel, Angel of Blessings, leader of--"

"An *angel*?"

Wyatt nodded. "I didn't believe it at first, either. I thought Gabriel was full of--"

"Is she Gabriel from the *Bible*?"

"Yeah."

"Holy crap."

"That's what *I* said."

"She's a big deal."

"She knows it, too, believe me."

"So, am I an angel, too?"

"Half," Wyatt told him. "Your mother was human. It shouldn't have been possible for you to be born. You're a miracle."

"So, I have your light-from-the-hands power, but--"

"Electricity. We can use the energy around us to create lightning. Now that you have the ability, I'll have to train you on how to control it."

"But, inside, I'm human?"

"Yeah, you have a proper human soul. You're a person like you've always been. The thing is, though, that the angel part of you might be a little hard to manage."

"What do you mean?"

"It might feel overwhelming. Gabriel said you could get headaches, have nightmares; even feel like you can't control yourself. These powers can make us dangerous to other people. If you ever feel like you can't handle it, if you feel yourself slipping, you have to tell me."

Will looked behind him into the living room, the broken furniture and boarded up doorway filling him with shame. "I didn't mean to--"

"Hey," Wyatt said, reaching his hand out and patting his son's arm. "I know that. Tonight, we'll clean up this mess. Tomorrow, we start training. A big part of controlling your lightning is knowing how to suppress it. That'll be lesson number one."

"Okay, Dad," Will said, picking up his soda can and taking a sip. He put it down and looked at his father. "*Angels?*"

Chapter 7

A strange man left Gabriel's apartment, passing Lucifer on his way to the elevator. As Lucifer went to open the door, it flew open in front of him, a beautiful woman also leaving, winking at him as she passed.

"Holy fuck buckets, that really watered my crops," Gabriel said, taking a water from the fridge, wearing only a thin, silk robe.

"I've only been gone a few hours. How did you manage to--" Lucifer stopped himself, realizing he had no interest in his sister's extracurricular activities. "Never mind."

"Don't go all 'Uriel' on me."

"Wouldn't dream of it. I just never understood the attraction to men." He sat at the bar, picking up the book he'd left there.

"Except you always choose a man to occupy when you're here."

"Yes, because I wish to indulge in the female body. This," he said, gesturing to himself. "Is purely for function."

"The functionality of the male body is precisely why I like it. And, FYI, most of the time, a woman better satisfies another woman than a man because she knows what feels good. Something to think about before your next trip topside."

"I'll take it under advisement."

Gabriel slammed her water bottle down and lifted Lucifer from his seat. "You have heroin?!" she accused, reaching into his pants pocket and pulling out the tiny bag of powder.

"Is that what it is? I took it off a demon after I sent him packing. He was so calm while I removed him. Piqued my curiosity."

Gabriel stormed through the hall and into the bathroom, tossing the bag into the toilet and flushing it.

"Well, that was rather rude," Lucifer complained.

"Don't bring that shit into my house."

"Why so vexed, sister? It was only for fun. Why should my experimentation irk you so?"

"You don't know everything about me." She charged past him, following the sound of her ringing phone. She took and quickly ended the call. "I'm gonna take a shower, then I have an errand to run."

"Does your errand have something to do with that phone call?"

"Yes."

"Might I join?"

"No."

"This is the thing," Gabriel said, plopping herself down to sit next to Allydia on her bed, the faint smell of death floating up from the decaying vampire as she remained unmoved. "When I get a call from a twenty-year-old ginger vampire, hysterically sobbing into the phone, making it impossible to understand what she's saying through her already barely coherent Scottish accent, I feel compelled to come see exactly what the fuck. Now, I've already been down here twice in the last week; this is getting ridiculous. They told me you took your feeding tube out as soon as I left. You know this behavior is--"

"Go away, Gabriel," Allydia said, her voice weak.

"Can't do it. If I let you die, my brother would be hella salty."

"Your brother doesn't care for me," the vampire bemoaned, tears forming in her eyes. "He disappeared. No explanation, no goodbye."

"About that, he left because I told him to go. It had nothing to do with you."

"You what?" Allydia hissed, struggling to set herself up.

"Can you keep a secret?"

Allydia nodded, her despair replaced with anger.

"He had a kid. Shouldn't have happened. I still don't know how it did. *I* don't know. Craziness. Turns out his wife left him because she was pregnant and thought he'd mess the kid up somehow."

Horror spread across Allydia's face. "A Nephilim?"

"Totes magotes. Which is why I made him leave the city, take that thing to the middle of nowhere, and hope nothing bad happens, but you remember what they're like. No way he grows up functional. He's been a good kid, though, so far. Sweet as can be. I love that little monstrosity."

"You allow the child to live?"

"Against my better judgement. I was kind of hoping Barachiel was right about him. That he might not ever get powers. But he did. He killed a *werewolf.*"

"A werewolf? That takes me back."

"Right? The kid's emotional, undisciplined. B's trying to teach him to control it, but you know as well as I do--"

"There is no controlling a Nephilim."

"Nope."

"You should have killed him when he was an infant."

"You think so? How do you think my brother would've reacted? You think he would've forgiven me? Because I don't."

"He would understand, eventually."

"The way you understand what Lilith did?"

"You know that's different."

"He wouldn't see it that way," Gabriel said, opening Allydia's nightstand drawer and pulling out a pen and a sheet of paper. "*Barachiel* would understand. *Barachiel* would probably thank me. But *Wyatt*? That motherfucker would set my bony ass on fire." She scribbled down an address and handed it to the vampire. "I'm trusting you'll keep your mouth shut. Lucifer's back and you know what he'll do if he finds out there's a Nephilim running around."

"I remember."

"All right, I'm gonna go, but for real, get it together. You're a goddamn queen. Take a shower, put on something fabulous, maybe a little blush for color. I don't want to be a dick, but you look like shit. And for fuck's sake, bitch, eat something."

Gabriel brushed by Hattie on her way out the door.

"Hattie, dear," Allydia called. The young vampire rushed to the queen's room.

"Yes, Your Majesty?"

"Be a lamb and run me a hot bath. While I wait, bring me a blood bag...or ten."

Chapter 8

Abaddon stared from the edge of the bed in the rundown motel room at the blurry television screen, the local news informing him of just how evil mankind still was. Arson, theft, and murder; so many murders. Every day there was something new for him to be incensed by. War, corruption, greed. It turned his stomach, now that he had one. The body he'd chosen had taken a bit of getting used to. It required food, water, and sleep, not things he'd taken into consideration before having made the journey to Earth. It felt confining and rigid. He'd been watching people on television, studying their movements and vernacular, waiting until he felt well enough acclimated to venture out without being noticed. Lucifer would have undoubtedly followed him, after pushing back the resistance among the damned, and Abaddon had research to do before forming a plan, let alone enacting one. Blending in was the priority for now.

The news was horrifying, but he still wasn't sure if humanity as a whole needed to be wiped clean from the Earth or if there were some people worth saving. He needed more data before making a final decision and he knew just where to go first to get it. Several commercials aired on cable news, each more obnoxious than the last, but one seemed to run more frequently than the rest. It was for a department store that sold everything from groceries to power tools. The ads always showed the inside of the store crawling with people, filling their carts with all manner of items, from the sensible to the absurd. He would go there now to observe more closely what had become of humanity since last he was corporeal.

"Well, aren't you fancy?" the older woman asked as he walked into the store. "Coming from work?"

"Always working," Abaddon answered, perplexed by the strangers greeting. She smiled as if to prove herself friendly, yet her comment on his appearance felt insulting somehow. He adjusted his suit jacket and glanced around, noticing immediately that he did seem overdressed for the setting. Most people wore shorts or jeans and tee-shirts. A few of the women wore sundresses. He realized his mistake. He'd dressed like the anchors on the news, not like the people in the commercials. He felt an odd sense of insecurity as he walked through the aisles, the puzzled looks on people's faces as he passed making him self-conscious. He straightened his tie and smoothed his lapels, the urge to do something with his hands overwhelming.

"Can I help you, sir?" a young man in a vest asked. He wore a name tag, indicating that he worked there, giving Abaddon a false sense of familiarity with the boy.

"Yes," he told the clerk. "How many people would you say the average person kills in their lifetime?"

"What? None."

"None?" Abaddon asked in disbelief. "Your news programs tell a different story."

"Look, man, I know you're not from around here, but--"

"What do you mean? How do you know that?"

"Uh, your accent, dude."

"What accent?"

"The British one."

"What is 'British'?"

"Listen, buddy, not all Americans are murderers. We don't all have guns and we don't all hate this race or that religion. The ones that do are just real loud."

"I see," Abaddon said. "And you yourself have never killed anyone?"

"Of course not, man!"

"Huh. Interesting."

"Do you need help finding something, or what?"

"Do you sell history books here?"

"Not really. There are a few on the website, but if you want to save some money, just check out Wikipedia or go to a library."

"And what is a Wikipedia and where is this place you call 'library'?"

The clerk glared at him. "Bro."

Abaddon scoured the history section of the library, nearly overwhelmed by the number of books on the subject. To make it more manageable, he started with American history, since he happened to be in the United States. He'd follow that with English history, since he, apparently, was speaking with an English accent, and go from there. He'd read every history book in the library. He wanted to get as much information on the evolution of the human species as he could. Perhaps if he understood *why* they behaved the way they did, he wouldn't have to slaughter them en masse. After all, the boy at the department store wasn't altogether awful, though maybe a tad condescending. Also, the woman that helped him find the history section of the library was quite pleasant and everyone in the building was polite and quiet. He gathered the books and sat at a table, noticing the sense of calm in the room as people minded their own business, only whispering when speaking at all. He liked it here.

He began reading a book detailing the American Revolution. It was brutal. It started with people being treated unfairly by their government and ended with approximately fifty-thousand people dead from battle wounds and disease. Men were taken prisoner, never to be heard from again. Cities devastated by fire. Children orphaned.

He continued reading, books chronicling The War of 1812 and The American Civil War. He was disgusted and outraged. He read about children working in factories, men dying in mines, and women burning alive in a garment factory, having been locked in their workrooms for no other reason than the greed of the men that owned the building. More wars followed, as did criminal leaders and assassinations. Terrorism, bombings…it was too much to take.

He decided to move on to English history, the country the Americans found too cruel to remain subject to. He thought there was no way they could have been as bloodthirsty and devious as the Americans. He soon discovered that the English were, in fact, even worse. The Crusades, Colonization, the many, many wars…the slave trade. He'd had enough. People throughout history had proven themselves evil beyond measure. He sat back in his seat, arms crossed, reflecting on what he'd learned. His stomach was in knots, rage mingled with something else. What was it? He couldn't remember the feeling. He then felt a warm tear slip down his cheek and he realized, it was sorrow. Sadness filled his chest as he covered his mouth, not wanting to bother anyone with the sound of his weeping. This is what humanity had come from; violence, injustice, malice. No wonder they still displayed such savagery. He wiped the tears from his face, put the books back where he'd found them, and headed toward the door. He'd come back tomorrow and learn the histories of African and Middle Eastern countries. Those were places he remembered as thriving and peaceful, for the most part. Surely, their stories would be easier to take than the ones he read today.

Chapter 9

"Dad!" Wyatt was jolted out of bed by the volume of the word. "Dad!" It was coming from the bathroom across the hall. The overhead light exploded. "DAD!" He opened the door and was taken aback by what he saw. It was Will, but it wasn't. Though his growth had always been accelerated, it had also been steady; subtle enough that Wyatt felt he was watching his son mature into every age. This was like nothing he'd seen before. Last night, Will went to bed a sixteen or so-year-old-boy. Today, he'd woken up a man in his mid-twenties. Wyatt was speechless.

"What happened to me, Dad?!" Will shouted, the lights above the mirror flickering.

Wyatt got his bearings and took his son's face in his hands, studying the changes that had occurred. It was like looking in a mirror to the past. He looked exactly like Wyatt's younger self, the resemblance to Annie all but gone. "It looks like you grew up."

"Overnight?!"

"Apparently. You okay? How do you feel?"

"Old."

Wyatt laughed and hugged him, Will trembling in his father's arms. "You're okay," Wyatt told him before calling to Gabriel. *Will looks twenty-five. Is that what's supposed to happen?*

Using his powers probably triggered a growth spurt, she answered. *He's done growing and I know you know what that means. Keep a real close eye on him. If he gets out of control--*

I know.

He pat Will's shoulder and looked him in the eyes. "We'll have to work hard to make sure you can control your powers and *yourself*. Lightning training every day.

Maybe some meditation or something to keep you calm when you start to feel stressed or angry."

Will nodded in agreement.

"The good news," Wyatt said. "Is that you'll age like everyone else from now on. If someone comes to the door--"

"No more hiding?" Will asked, his anxiety giving way to hope.

"No more panicking at the sight of people," Wyatt corrected. "As far as going out, I don't know--"

"Come on, Dad. What's the worst that could happen?"

"Power outages, electrical fires, death and destruction."

"Dad,"

"All right, listen, I have some paperwork at the shop I need to deal with. I'll only be there for an hour or so. The truth is, I don't want to leave you alone right now, so you can come with me, but if you start feeling--"

"If I get overwhelmed, we'll come home. I get it."

"Do you? Because it's the most important thing in the world as far as you're concerned. With our powers, things can go from zero to Apocalypse in seconds."

"I understand, Dad. I promise I won't put anyone in danger."

"All right," Wyatt said, still unsure if bringing him along was the right thing to do.

"Thanks, Dad. What's for breakfast? I feel like I haven't eaten in a week."

Wyatt laughed as they headed down the stairs. "Oh, and Will, if anyone asks, I had you when I was a teenager."

"Your office is smaller than I thought," Will said, looking with interest around the room. "Offices on TV are big, have windows and plants. This is a dungeon with a desk."

"Hey," Wyatt chuckled. "I also have a safe and a file cabinet, so, you know, I'm living the dream." He went back to filling out purchase orders, not noticing his son peeking out into the shop.

So many people, Will thought. He watched them like a movie as they ate, stood in line, and spoke to one another. Being out in the world again was exhilarating. He could feel the energy coming from the room just beyond the door. It was magnetic. He wanted desperately to be part of it, to be among the people. Then, he saw her.

"Dad!" he whispered. "That's her! That's the girl from the SATs. I didn't know she worked here."

Wyatt got up from his seat and peered through the crack in the door. "I haven't seen her before. She must be the new cashier Charlie hired."

Will abruptly closed the door. "Am I attractive?" he asked.

"I'm sorry, what?"

"Am I good-looking? I mean, you see her, she's gorgeous. Do I have a chance?"

"I don't know how to answer this question."

"Should I ask for her number?" Will wondered. "Am I allowed to date? What do people even *do* on dates?"

"Slow down," Wyatt instructed. "Breathe. Don't worry about dating just yet. You haven't even introduced yourself. As far as she knows, you're a complete stranger."

"Right," Will realized. "The guy she met at the high school was ten years younger."

"Exactly, so don't freak her out by asking for a date first thing. Girls don't like to feel ambushed. You can't just walk up to her and ask for her number. You have to be casual. Have a normal conversation."

"Okay," Will said. "Yeah, just talk to her like a normal person. Except *I don't talk to people, Dad.* What do I say?"

"Hi."

"Dad,"

"You say, 'hi'. Let her take your order. If she's interested, she'll give you an indication. Prolonged eye contact, smiling, touching her hair. Now, some of that is just being friendly or even just polite because she's working in customer service, so don't get your hopes up. Ask a question. Nothing personal, just small talk. See how the conversation goes. Tell a joke. If she laughs, you have a shot. If she touches your arm, she's most likely into you. Don't ask for her number. It's not like you'll never see her again, she works here. Give her space so she feels comfortable."

"Okay," Will said. "Solid advice. Insightful."

"Thank you."

"How'd you get so good at this?"

"Practice."

"You had a lot of girlfriends?"

"In my younger days."

"What happened?"

"Don't worry about it."

"Come to think of it, have you been on a date since Mom--"

"Are you gonna talk to the girl, or not?"

"Yeah," Will nodded. He took a deep breath and let it out slowly. "Okay. I'm going for it." The two stood, neither of them moving an inch.

"Soon?" Wyatt teased.

"I just need a second." Will cracked the door and looked out into the room. The line had dwindled and Michelle had no customers. "Okay, I'm going."

He nervously approached the counter, glancing back at his father who gave him a reassuring nod. Wyatt closed the door, wondering if he'd made a mistake letting Will go. On one hand, he was a grown man now, and keeping him locked up at home seemed barbaric and slightly abusive. On the other hand, he knew what his son was capable of and while he'd shown no signs of being unnecessarily angry or otherwise insane, his personality could turn on a dime, according to Gabriel, who had been right about everything else, so far. He leaned against the door, uncertainty taking hold, and said to himself, "Parenting is hard."

Michelle struggled to get the coin wrapper open, the roll of quarters slippery in her hands. As she finally made some progress at ripping the paper, the whole thing fell apart, spewing coins in all directions.

"Come on," she whispered, crouching on the floor to pick up the rogue change. She looked up, seeing a man also crouching on the other side of the glass donut case in front of her. As the two stood, Michelle quickly noticed how cute he was. Dark eyes and hair, kind of tall, wearing a tee-shirt that seemed a touch too big for him. He moved awkwardly, as if nervous, which endeared him to her even more.

"You dropped these," the young man said, placing the three quarters he'd picked up on the counter.

She took them and put them in her drawer, hoping she'd found them all. "Thanks."

"Don't worry," he said. "I didn't take any."

"Oh, I know," she said, not actually knowing that at all, but feeling compelled to put him at ease. "What can I get you?"

"Um, two glazed, please."

As she reached for the donuts, she could see him fidgeting with the empty coin wrapper, signaling to her that he was anxious to speak to her. It was precious.

"You don't have to be nervous," she told him, placing the donuts in a bag.

"What? I'm not, I mean, it's just,"

"Just what?"

"I'm sorry, I'm trying to think of something funny to say, but you're so, you're..."

"I'm what?"

"You're just so pretty. Sorry, I'm probably staring like a creep. I'll leave you alone." He paid for the donuts and took the bag, sure he'd blown it. He started to walk off, but she called him back.

"Hey," she said, writing her cell number on the coin wrapper. "I'm Michelle. We should hang out sometime." He took the paper, a tingling sensation building in his stomach.

"Cool," he said, the delight in his voice evident. "I'll call you. Tomorrow. I'll call you tomorrow."

"Hey," she called after him as he headed to the back of the shop. "What's your name?"

"It's Will. Will Sinclair," he called back, disappearing into the owner's office.

Her heart sank. "Oh, fuck me," she said under her breath.

"She gave me her number!" Will said, showing Wyatt the torn wrapper.

"That's great," Wyatt said, trying to cover his apprehension and sound supportive. "What are you gonna do now?"

"Eat these donuts and have a mild panic attack."

Chapter 10

Will looked down at the skates, now securely tied. He'd never worn skates before, let alone been to a roller rink, but it's what Michelle had suggested they do and he couldn't refuse her. Something about her smile made him weak and when she took his hand to help him to his feet, he thought he might faint.

"You okay?" she asked, now holding onto both of his hands to keep him steady, her soft skin giving him chills.

"Yeah, I'm fine," he said, shaking, trying hard not to fall.

Michelle laughed. "Maybe we should stay in the arcade area for a while. It has carpet."

"Let's do that," Will said, unable to hide the relief in his voice. "I'll get some quarters." He awkwardly scooted himself to the change machine and put in a five-dollar bill. He gave twelve quarters to Michelle and pocketed the rest.

"Thank you, Will. That's nice of you," she told him.

"If three dollars in change impresses you, wait til I buy you nachos later."

"I will never not be impressed by nachos."

"And cotton candy."

"Now you're just showing off."

The two played for about an hour, beating each other in several racing games. The building was relatively quiet for a Friday night, only a couple dozen people on the rink itself and less than a handful in the arcade. The restaurant area was nearly empty when they sat down to eat.

"As promised," Will said, setting the plate of nachos in front of his date as she took a sip of soda.

"And you're officially the coolest person I know in this town," she complimented. He gave a shy laugh and sat, his own nachos beckoning him like sirens. He shoveled them into his mouth a few at a time, paying no mind to the cheese dripping to his chin.

"Hungry?" Michelle asked.

"Always." He drank his soda and sat quietly while Michelle ate. *Ask questions*, his father had told him. *Be interested. Listen.* "So, what did you do before you started working at Pine's?"

"I was a personal assistant."

"What was that like?" he asked, wiping the cheese from his face with a napkin.

"It was a lot of work," she told him, remembering the long hours of martial arts training. "But, I learned a ton. My old boss knows all kinds of interesting stuff. And she's not a bad time to be around. She's real funny."

"Why'd you leave?"

She knew she couldn't tell him the truth, but she felt strangely guilty about lying to him, so she compromised. "It was just time for me to get out of New York."

"New York? That's where my dad's from. What's it like?"

"Busy."

"A lot of people, right?"

"Yeah."

"I've always wanted to go, but it's probably not in the cards," Will said, the disappointment in his voice apparent. "At least, not for a while."

"Why not?" Michelle reflexively asked, already knowing the answer.

"Being around a lot of people is, um...worrisome."

"Oh."

"I mean, I like people. I don't have social anxiety or anything, it's just," he paused for a moment, trying to think of how best to explain it to her without revealing too much. "Growing up, I had to stay away from people because my dad was worried they wouldn't understand me. I had a condition. Now, I just really hope I am who I think I am."

"Well, not that my opinion means anything, but you seem okay to me."

"Your opinion means *everything*."

She stopped eating, a twinge of emotion bubbling up in her stomach. She was crushing hard, a direct violation of the rules. She wasn't even supposed to have a conversation with Will that went beyond small talk, let alone be on a date with him. She watched him as he smiled at her, taking her trash to the garbage before heading back to the concession stand to buy dessert. She knew Gabriel would be pissed, so she decided not to get too attached. *Keep it casual*, she thought, deciding there was no harm in befriending him, as long as that's as far as it went. *No kissing*, she vowed, but as he walked back to the table, cotton candy in hand, she knew she was kidding herself. Besides being the first guy to show any real interest in her, he was cute as could be, smart and charming. No one had ever looked at her the way he did, like she could do no wrong, and as he handed her the cotton candy, a tiny static shock passing between them, butterflies in her stomach, she thought, *I'm fucked*.

Wyatt drained the hamburger he'd browned and returned it to the pan. Will would be back any second and he wanted to surprise him with a special meal to either celebrate his first date or comfort him if it had gone badly. He'd put the pan back on the stove when he felt an eerie sensation, compelled to look out the window above the sink. It was dark and he could barely make out the shadowy form of the barn at the back of the yard and the treeline just past it. Nothing seemed out of the ordinary, but he was sure something was off.

As he reached for the back door's knob, he heard the front door close. He went to the living room to find Will back home.

"How was it?" Wyatt asked.

"Amazing," Will said, locking the door behind him. "She's amazing. She's funny and interesting and, jeez, Dad, she's so pretty. I probably freaked her out staring so much."

Wyatt laughed. "I'm glad you had a good time."

"I had a *great* time. One thing, though. Can you teach me how to drive? It's kind of embarrassing being twenty-five with no license. I don't want her to think I'm weird."

"Sure," Wyatt agreed. "We'll have to start lessons next weekend, though. I have to go to the city for a couple of days. There's food in the kitchen and I'll leave you some money for pizza. You think you can handle being here alone until Monday?"

"Sure."

"While I'm gone, no powers, okay? We can get back to practicing when I get home, but I don't want there to be any mistakes, you understand?"

"I get it, Dad. I'll be fine."

"All right."

"I get why I can't go with you," Will said. "But will I be able to someday? Go to New York? See where you're from, where you met Mom?"

"Of course," Wyatt said, putting his hand on his son's shoulder. "You're doing well controlling your abilities and being out in public. No incidents, so far. I think with a few more months of training and meditation, you'll be ready to live a normal life like everyone else."

"I hope so. I'd like to see what all the fuss is about. New York, I mean. Not a normal life. Although, that too, to be honest."

Wyatt laughed again, heading to the kitchen. "You hungry? I'm making tacos."

"You're *what*?"

"I can make tacos."

"Since when?"

"Since college. I just don't do it very often."

"I have no recollection of you ever--"

"Do you want tacos, or not?"

Will nodded.

Wyatt got a box of shells from the pantry and read the instructions. Will could see the concentration on his father's face and decided it would most likely be a while before dinner would be ready, so he went up to his room, sat on the end of his bed, and called Michelle.

"I just wanted to make sure you got home safe," he told her.

"I'm still driving," she said.

"Oh, right. I didn't-- hey, would it be weird if I asked you out again? Is it too soon? You had a good time, right?"

"I had a really good time."

"My dad's going out of town, so I should probably stay in, but maybe you could come over? We could watch TV or something."

"I'll bring some DVDs," Michelle agreed. "There's an awesome show that's like, mandatory viewing. See you Sunday?"

"Sunday's perfect! Listen, I'm sorry if I made you uncomfortable tonight. I didn't mean to stare."

"You didn't."

"Oh, good. You're just...I really like you."

There was a long pause.

"Michelle? Are you there?"

"I'm here," she said.

"Sorry. Did I freak you out? Am I coming on too strong? I shouldn't have said any--"

"I like you, too, Will."

"Oh," he said, relief washing over him. "Thank you. I mean, good. I mean--"

"Can I call you back when I get home? It's starting to rain and I should concentrate on the road."

"Oh, yeah, of course. I'll talk to you later."

"Okay, bye."

"Bye." He put the phone down and fell back onto his bed. He couldn't stop smiling, Michelle's voice lingering in his mind. *I like you, too.* It was the most beautiful thing he'd ever heard.

"Will! Dinner!" Wyatt called.

Will jumped up, the smell of taco seasoning filling his nose. As he raced down the stairs, he couldn't help but say, out loud, "Best day ever."

Later that night, Michelle called back and they talked for hours about everything from the crazy Indiana weather to their mother's deaths. They had so much in common including their tastes in music, food and never feeling like they belonged anywhere besides home. Will was thoroughly smitten and after their conversation, he was sure she was super into him, too.

Will sat in the silence, the empty house feeling bigger with his father gone. He had been reading, but his mind wandered to thoughts of Michelle. They had plans for the next day to binge episodes of a show he'd never heard of that she swore was incredible. It would be only them, together, in the house, alone. He was nervous, so he put the book down and opened the laptop. *What to do when you're alone with a girl*, he searched. "Nope," he said, closing the window that had become covered in pornographic imagery. He knew from several awkward conversations with his dad that porn and real-life rarely had anything in common. Besides, he wasn't expecting things to move that quickly with Michelle. He was just hoping for some helpful tips on how to behave that were more specific than the 'just be yourself' speech his dad had given him. He closed the computer, dissatisfied with what he found on the subject, and took a sip of water before placing the bottle back on the kitchen table. He glanced up at the window, noticing the storm raging outside. Hail the size of golf balls was raining down so hard, it put a dent in the grill. The sky was dark and swirling, the angry clouds looking lower to the ground than usual. Then, he heard it... the siren. As he started to head to the basement, a knock came on the front door. He wasn't sure if he should answer it. Normally, he would hide until the person left, but a person shouldn't be out in this weather, so he hesitantly opened the door.

"Michelle," he greeted. "I thought you were coming over tomorrow."

"I am," she said, grateful to be under the porch and out of the hail. "But, my apartment doesn't have a basement and I'm not used to this weather. Would it be okay if--"

"Of course!" he blurted, stepping aside to let her in. "Come in. I was just about to head downstairs." They hurried to the basement, Will turning on the dim overhead light before joining Michelle on the old, dusty sofa. They watched the hail pile up outside the small windows near the ceiling, both of them feeling anxious, but for different reasons.

"So, this happens a lot here?" she asked.

"No, just like, twenty or so times a year."

"Oh, is that all?" she giggled.

"It's not that bad. I've lived here my whole life and have never had anything particularly bad happen because of a storm."

"Okay," she said, her shoulders relaxing. "That makes me feel a little better."

"The good thing about tornadoes is that even if they're right on top of you, they're gone in like, two minutes."

"Yeah. You're right. We should maybe try not to think about it. So, what have you been up to today?"

"Reading some Dickens. What about you?"

"Ignoring friend requests and blocking people on social media."

"Why?"

"People in high school weren't exactly nice to me. There was a lot of racism and at the time, I ignored it, but these people all of a sudden out of nowhere deciding they want to be friends or whatever is...like, I want to ask them if they're lost."

"I'm so sorry. I can't imagine what that must have been like for you."

"Yeah, you're pretty white." They both laughed before she spoke again. "It's just hard when you already don't feel Black enough or Asian enough and then you have all these white kids calling you 'ugly' and on top of it, the Dean is--"

"Ugly?!" Will interrupted.

"Yeah. I mean, I know I shouldn't listen to tha--"

"You are the furthest thing from ugly. You're so far from ugly, ugly couldn't see you with a telescope. *You*, you're the most beautiful girl I've ever seen. *Ever*. And that includes lingerie models I saw on a TV special once."

"That's nice of you to say," she told him, pushing her hair behind her ear.

"I mean it. You're *gorgeous*. Anyone that would say otherwise is either lying or needs glasses."

"Thanks," she said, her insecurities giving way to something else. The somewhat manageable crush she had before was growing stronger and as she looked into his eyes, she felt the will to hold herself back leave her. Before she knew what she was doing, she leaned in and kissed him. He was surprised, then delighted. He'd never kissed anyone before and it was everything he'd thought it would be and more. Not wanting it to end, he took her face in his hands, letting them wander into her hair and back. He felt warm all over like he'd been wrapped in a heated blanket. As the world fell away, the light above flickered, then went out completely. They didn't notice.

Chapter 11

"Look at you, you gorgeous bitch," Gabriel beamed.

"I know, right?" Valerie said, checking herself out in the mirror. "Get back here and zip me up. It's almost time." Gabriel complied then hugged her sister from behind.

"I'm really happy for you," she told her. "Malik's a good dude, not to mention sexy as fuck. Honestly, nice haul."

"Girl, I will hurt you."

"May I come in?" Lucifer called from the other side of the dressing room door.

"Yeah!" Gabriel called back, ignoring Valerie's annoyed glare.

"Well, you look lovely, Uriel," Lucifer said as he entered the room. "I just wanted to give you my gift now as I'll be leaving after the ceremony to attend to more pressing matters. Congratulations." He handed her an envelope. "I've booked you a honeymoon in Venice. I haven't been there myself in a few hundred years, but the travel agent assured me that its retained it's romantic ambiance. Do mind the ghosts."

"Thank you, Lucifer. That's actually very sweet," Valerie said, surprised by his kindness.

"Thank Gabriel. It was her money I spent."

"You know I give zero fucks about money," Gabriel interjected. "If I did, I'd give you a lecture on the benefits of *free* internet porn. My credit card statement looks like I live with a teenage boy on Rumspringa."

"All right, let's not make me throw up while I'm in my dress, okay? Thank you," Valerie cringed.

"For real," Gabriel continued. "You should hit that bartender chick up. Get it out of your system."

"I will consider it," Lucifer told her. "And, I'll abstain from viewing certain websites, on the condition that you eat something green that grew from the ground every day."

"That's...you know what? Look at whatever porn you want. It's none of my business."

Lucifer smirked. "I will go take my seat now," he said, leaving the room.

"Hey, can I talk to you for a second?" Valerie asked.

"About the kid thing?" Gabriel asked.

"Yeah. Can you get in Malik's head and see if he-- I mean, he knows I can't have kids, but I think he wants them."

"He does."

"Fuck."

"It's cool. I put a hundred thousand dollars in your checking account this morning."

"Bitch, you did what?"

"Happy wedding!"

"Girl,"

"Adoption's expensive, plus you'll have to buy a crib and diapers and shit."

"It's too much."

"A, no it's not, and two, what we are shouldn't prohibit you from living your life. Don't forget, I know what you want. I know you better than you know yourself. You deserve everything good in the world and it would make me happy to make you happy. So, quit being stubborn and take the fucking money. And, thank your lucky stars I didn't give you more, because I wanted to, but I knew what kind of fit you'd throw."

"I don't kno--"

"Just accept my love!"

"Fine, Jesus," Valerie chuckled. "But I hope you don't think I'll be asking you to babysit."

Gabriel scoffed. "You better not. I am not equipped."

"And, now that I'm all in my dress, *of course,* I have to pee." Valerie shooed Gabriel from the room for privacy.

"It's not like I haven't seen it!" Gabriel called through the door.

"Bitch, stay out of my head!"

Gabriel waited impatiently, looking onto the crowd of people, trying to block out the thoughts of Valerie's coworkers and college friends. Each one saw her slightly differently. To some, she was the reliable friend that got them home safely after happy hour. To others, she was someone they could trust to give them the best advice. To her college roommate, she was the straight girl she still had feelings for but never had the guts to tell. Gabriel wouldn't spill the woman's secret; it would only make things awkward and she knew how much her friendship meant to her sister.

"Barachiel," Gabriel whispered to herself, feeling him enter the building. She rushed to find him placing a package on the gift table. "B!" she nearly shouted, throwing her arms around his neck and hugging him tightly.

"Gabriel," he said, a broad smile covering his face. "How are you?"

"Awesome," she said, pulling away to look at his face. "First, I want you to know that I've missed you terribly, but also," She smacked his arm hard.

"Ow!" he laughed.

"You let him kill the werewolf?" she whispered.

"I didn't *let* him. The thing was killing me. He got scared. And why could he kill it, but I couldn't? I gave that thing everything I had and it didn't make a dent."

"Because he's stronger than you, stupid. You have to pull energy from somewhere else. Static in the air, light sockets, the atmosphere. Meanwhile, Will has a battery inside him with more power than the goddamn sun. A human soul is condensed creation. Nothing in the universe is stronger than that but God, and He's on vacation. That's what makes Will so dangerous."

"He's not dangerous," Wyatt insisted.

"Are you sure? Because if he goes dark side, you won't be able to control him."

"He's fine."

"Wyatt!" Valerie squealed, hurrying to give her brother a quick hug. "I'm digging the suit. You clean up nice."

"Congratulations," he told her.

"Thank you, thank you."

"Gabriel tells me Malik's a decent guy."

"He's perfection personified. Listen, I was wondering since I don't have a daddy or anything if you'd walk me down the aisle? I know we haven't seen each other in a minute, but--"

"I'd be honored."

"That's good because it's time to start. Go ahead, girl. Kick this shit off." They headed to the ceremony room and paused outside the entrance, Valerie jumping in her skin as she took her brother's arm. Gabriel walked to the rose petal-covered aisle runner and waited for the music to start. When it did, she took one slow step after another toward the arch at the other end where the minister, Malik, and his best man stood. She took her place and listened to Valerie's fiance's thoughts.

Who is this white boy walking her down the aisle? Must be one of her foster brothers. Damn, she looks good. I can't wait to get my hands on her tonight.

Ew. Gabriel thought.

What is this music? Lucifer asked.

The Wedding March of Osterdalen, Gabriel answered. *I thought you'd appreciate it.*

Wyatt left Valerie at the altar and took his seat next to Lucifer.

"Nice to see you, brother," Lucifer greeted.

"Lucifer."

"Does this song remind you of anything?"

"It's vaguely familiar," he admitted. "I can't place it."

"We heard something like it once at a wedding in Norway. Let's hope this one ends differently."

"Oh. I'm sorry, I don't remember that."

"It's probably for the best. This version of you probably wouldn't have the stomach for what came after the music ended."

"We've gathered here today," the minister began. "To celebrate the joining of this man and this woman in Holy Matrimony. If anyone here objects to this union, please speak now, or forever hold your peace."

Lucifer jokingly whispered, "Should I--"

"You better not," Wyatt warned.

"If there are no objections, we'll begin," the minister continued. "The couple have written their own vows." He gestured to Valerie to start. She nodded and looked into Malik's eyes. He could see how nervous she was, so he took her hands in his and offered a reassuring smile. She smiled back and cleared her throat before speaking.

"Love is patient. Love is kind. I'm neither of those things." The crowd quietly laughed as she continued. "But, I promise that I'll try, every day, to be whatever it is you need me to be. If you're upset, I'll comfort you. If you're sick, I'll heal you. If you're hungry, let's be honest, you'll probably have to feed yourself, but I can set a table like nobody's business." Malik and the crowd laughed again. "Seriously, though, you're the best man I've ever known and I'll do everything I can to always make you happy. I love you."

"Thank you, Valerie," the minister said as Malik kissed her hands. "Now, Malik."

"Valerie Moore," Malik said. "You are crazy and wild. You're argumentative and stubborn and you always have to have things your way." Again, the crowd chuckled. "And I have loved every second of being with you. You make me laugh. You make me whole. The light you bring into my life has made me a better man. You, Ms. Moore, are the absolute best thing that God has been gracious enough to bless me with and I will spend the rest of my life working to be the man you deserve. I love you more and more every minute of every day. Thank you for the honor of allowing me in your life."

Smooth, Gabriel thought.

Isn't he, though? Valerie responded.

"And now," the minister said. "The rings." Malik's best man gave him the white gold band. "Repeat after me. With this ring, I thee wed."

"With this ring," Malik repeated, slipping the ring on Valerie's finger. "I thee wed."

Gabriel handed Valerie Malik's ring. Again, the minister said, "Repeat after me. With this ring, I thee wed."

"With this ring," Valerie said, placing the ring on Malik's finger. "I thee wed."

"By the power vested in me by the Sikes Memorial Methodist Church and the state of New Jersey, I hereby pronounce you husband and wife. You may kiss your bride."

Malik kissed his new wife with a little more tongue than was appropriate as the attendants cheered. They turned to face the crowd, held hands, and gleefully jumped over the broom Malik's mother had placed on the floor, the guests again erupting in applause. They walked back down the aisle and into the ballroom as "That's How Strong My Love Is" by Otis Redding played overhead.

"Give our sisters my best, won't you?" Lucifer said quietly as he stood.

"You're not staying for the reception?" Wyatt asked.

"No time. While Gabriel, to my dismay, seems less than fully invested in the mission at hand, I intend on bringing Abaddon to justice in a much more timely fashion than we did Lilith. It really was good to see you, Barachiel. Perhaps, when the world as we know it is no longer in danger, we can catch up properly." He pat Wyatt on the back before moving past him to leave.

"Hey, you like Foo Fighters, right?" Gabriel asked on her way past Wyatt.

"Sure," he said, gently taking her arm to stop her.

"Good, because I have a surprise for Uriel. She has no idea--"

"Abaddon?" Wyatt interrupted. "Were you ever intending on filling me in?"

"No. It's not for you to worry about," she told him, pulling her arm away. "Unlike Lucifer's rowdy twin, Abaddon has no way of hiding where he is from me. Don't tell you-know-who. The wild goose chase is keeping him out of trouble, for now. I can't have him going on another murder spree."

"Gabriel,"

"Relax. I know what Abaddon's after and where he plans on getting it and he's not there yet. I'm keeping an eye on him, don't worry. I'm honestly trying to give him a chance to change his mind, redeem himself. It's probably not in the cards, though."

"Do you need any help?"

"Nah. You just have a good time at the reception, come back to my place for pizza and beer, and in a couple of days, go back to the sticks and make sure your spawn hasn't gone full psycho."

"Will is--"

"Nope," Gabriel stopped him, putting her hand up and turning her head. "I can't think about that right now. I have a party to get to."

"I'm fine, Dad," Will said.

"Are you sure?" Wyatt asked, his phone pressed to one ear and his hand to the other in a feeble attempt to block out the music blaring in the ballroom just beyond the doors where he stood, barely able to hear his son's responses to his questions.

"Yes, Dad. Nothing is gonna happen in two days."

"You remember what we talked about? If you ever feel like you're losing control--"

"Deep breaths, count to ten and call you right away. I know."

"And?"

"And no powers. I know all this, Dad. You don't have to worry about me. Go have some fun. You deserve a break. Spend some time with your sisters. I know you miss them."

"All right, call me if--"

"Bye, Dad."

"Bye." Wyatt ended the call and put his phone back in his jacket pocket. He knew he was being paranoid. Gabriel had gotten in his head, but Will was right. He *had* missed his sisters, more than he'd realized until he saw them again. "All Of Me" was over, which meant so was Valerie and Malik's first dance. Wyatt made his way to the ballroom where he saw Valerie and Gabriel dancing to a version of "In Da Club" he hadn't heard before and as he watched them, he felt calm, their happiness giving him a sense of well-being. If they could celebrate this unencumbered while Abaddon, whoever that was, was on the loose, he could relax a bit, too, for a change.

When the song ended, Gabriel ran to the DJ booth and took the microphone. "Can I get everyone's attention, please?" she piped. The room went quiet. "As some of you know, I'm Gabriel, Valerie's sister. For those of you that look confused, yes, we have different parents. Don't think about it too hard. So, when we were teenagers, we had pretty different tastes in music. Try as I might, I could never get her to like certain bands I was in to. One day, though, we were listening to a radio show that shall remain nameless and the guest played an acoustic version of my favorite song. By some miracle, Valerie loved it. About a decade later, they released that version on an album that I bought several copies of, and over the years, we've spent many nights eating junk and listening to that song on repeat. Just like that song, marriage is new to my girl, but I'm sure she'll love it just as much. Congratulations." She handed the mic back to the DJ as "Everlong" began to play. Suddenly, a curtain opened revealing a wall of windows showcasing a beautiful ocean view and something else.

"You didn't!" Valerie squealed among the gasps and cheers from the wedding guests.

"Bitch, you know that I did," Gabriel said, smiling wide as she gave her sister a hug. They listened intently until the song was over and applause broke out.

"Hey, Wyatt," Valerie said as he came to stand with his sisters. "Can't talk now. I'm gonna go meet Dave Grohl!" She rushed off toward the stage, leaving Wyatt and Gabriel alone.

"Impressive," he said.

"So, the kid says he's fine."

"Yeah."

"All right. If you trust him, I trust him." *Trust, but verify*, she thought as she checked her phone for messages from Michelle. Nothing new.

"Where'd your phone come from?" he wondered, noticing she wasn't carrying a bag.

"This dress has *pockets*!"

"If I eat any more, I'm gonna die of cheese," Gabriel complained.

Wyatt laughed, taking a final sip of beer before standing and putting the empty pizza box in the kitchen.

"Hey," Gabriel said, getting up from the sofa and following her brother, sitting at the bar and drinking the last of her soda. "I'm sorry I called Will psycho. Or said he *would be* psycho. Or whatever I said. You know I love that kid, right?"

"I know," Wyatt acknowledged, sitting across from her.

"I just worry."

"Yeah, well, so do I," he admitted. "He hasn't done anything to make me think he'll go dark side, as you put it, but when he killed the werewolf, I felt sick. I felt guilty. I should have been able to protect him from that. He's distracted right now since he's discovered girls, but I know it bothers him. It's a burden, the regret of what he did. He understands that he had to, but deep down--"

"He's not over it."

"No. And if he gets...if he loses control--"

"You're a good dad, B. Better than yours and light years better than mine. Who knows? Maybe he'll be fine. The Nephilim back in the day had no mothers and their fathers all left them before they were born. They had no one to teach them how to be what they were. You being around could be the thing Will needs to stay Will and keep him from flipping his shit."

"Do you believe that?"

"Fifty/fifty."

"That's encouraging."

"I'm going to bed. Your room's where you left it." She got up and headed down the hall. "Love you!" she called.

"Love you, too!" he called back, checking his phone before heading to bed himself. A text from Will sent a little over an hour before read *Going to bed. Night.*

Wyatt let out a sigh of relief as he put the phone down on the bar. Will was okay. Everything was okay.

Chapter 12

"Seven seasons," Michelle said excitedly. "A hundred and forty-four episodes."

"That's a lot," Will pointed out.

"That's just the beginning. There's a spin-off series almost as awesome. I brought those DVDs, too."

Will laughed. "There's no way we're getting through those today."

"No, but we can *start*. I'll leave everything here for you to watch when you feel like and we can talk about the episodes later. You ready?"

He nodded and handed her the remote. His arm felt like home to her as she wrapped it around her shoulders and snuggled in next to him. She couldn't help but dance a little in her seat as the show's theme played. They stayed there all day, watching hour after hour, eating candy, and cuddling on the couch. They'd gotten through the seventh episode when Will hit pause.

"So," he said. "She kills--"

"Yeah."

"But, she's in love with--"

"Yeah."

"That's gonna be awkward later."

"You don't even know."

"Does she kill him?"

"No spoilers!"

"Seems like a waste," he bemoaned. "Why have this whole love story if she just ends up killing him?"

"It's romantic."

"It's depressing."

"That's what romance is," she told him. "Romance can't exist without tragedy. How do you know if something was worth having if you've never felt the pain of losing it?"

"That's dark."

"That's life."

"What about happily ever after?"

"Like fairy tales?"

"No, like," he thought for a second. "Take Charlie, for example. She's been married to the same guy since she was eighteen. Their oldest kid is about to have a kid of her own. It's nice."

"Okay, but, best-case scenario, they're together until one of them dies, leaving the other one alone and miserable."

"Sure, everyone dies, but isn't it love that makes life worth living? Spending however long you have with someone that understands you and makes you feel--"

"Happy?"

"Worthy. Useful. Seen. Building a life and maybe a family with someone, feeling like you belong somewhere. 'Romeo and Juliet' isn't aspirational, it's *sad*. A little old lady and a little old man holding hands on their front porch while their grandkids play in the yard, *that's* something to strive for."

"God, you are just," She touched his cheek, letting herself fall into the whirlpool of his eyes. "So fucking awesome." She pressed her lips to his and climbed onto his lap, the heat between them rising like the tide. As they kissed, Will was overtaken by lust. He wrapped his arms around her and laid her down, the feeling of her beneath him the rightest thing he'd ever known. He moved from her lips to her neck, breathing her in like life. He then felt himself, now hard as stone, rub against her. Embarrassed, he backed away.

"I'm so sorry," he said, covering himself with a throw pillow. "I got carried away."

She slipped her jeans off, keeping her eyes locked on his. His heart pounded as she opened her legs in front of him.

"Are," he said, hardly able to speak. "Are you sure?"

She nodded.

He threw the pillow to the floor and tore his own pants off, never having moved that fast in his life. He climbed on top of her and asked again, "Are you sure?" Again, she nodded. He looked at her, honored and amazed that someone so incredible would be with him. He kissed her, all thoughts of restraint fleeing his mind like passengers on a sinking ship. He heard her take a sharp breath as he entered her. "Am I hurting you?" he asked.

"No," she assured him. "No, keep going." He obeyed, doing his best to be gentle. The sensations were overwhelming. The world went away. The room, the television, even the couch all disappeared. All he could feel was her engulfing him like a slow-moving hurricane. She was his entire universe. Her heavy breathing synced with his as he felt her pulse around him. He tried to stop himself from coming inside her, realizing he'd forgotten to use a condom, but he couldn't. He let out a breathy moan as he finished before again apologizing.

"I'm sorry. I forgot a condom."

"It's okay," she said, steadying her breathing. "I'll take care of it."

He brushed a few stray hairs away from her face and looked at her adoringly. "You're stunning."

"Am I romanticizing you or are you just like, the perfect man?"

"I don't know about perfect," he told her. "Happy, though. You make me feel...I can't explain it. You just, you make me *feel*. I'm so grateful for you, Michelle." A flood of emotion and hormones washed over them as they kissed, Will reentering her with more ease than before.

"Again?" she breathed.

"And again," he said, kissing her neck. "And again, and again."

Wyatt dropped his bag and closed the door behind him. "Will!" he called. As he entered the living room, he saw several cleaning products on the coffee table. He then saw what they were for. On the sofa was a large stain that could only have been made by one thing... blood. Wyatt's heart sank. "Will!" he called again.

"Hey, Dad," Will said, bounding down the stairs. "Don't worry, I'm cleaning it up right now. Nothing was working, so I looked it up. Supposedly, peroxide gets it out like magic." He opened the small bottle and dumped its contents onto the couch. The stain began to lighten. "Well, I'll be damned."

"What did you do, Will?" Wyatt asked, seeing that the boy wasn't hurt himself.

"Please don't freak out."

"What did you do?"

"I had sex. Are you mad? Oh, and I forgot to use a condom, but she took the morning after pill, so everything's fine. She didn't tell me until after that she was a virgin, too. I would've put a towel down or something."

"Oh, God," Wyatt said, relief replacing dread. He pulled his son in for a hug. "I thought something bad happened."

"You're not mad?"

"No, I'm just glad you're okay," Wyatt replied, patting him on the shoulder and stepping back.

"Good, because I have questions."

"I'm sure you do," Wyatt chuckled.

"What does love feel like?"

"Love? Don't you think it's a little early?"

"I have no idea, that's why I'm asking you. I haven't seen what a relationship is supposed to look like. You haven't dated anyone, as far as I know, my whole life, and you're my only role model, so--"

"All right," Wyatt said defensively. "I've had a little bit of a dry spell."

"Dry? Dad, there's more rain in the Sahara."

"Okay, just sit your ass down. I'm gonna give you an education." He took a DVD from the cabinet and put it in the player. "My wedding to your mother." He skipped ahead a few scenes. "Watch me when she's saying her vows. See that look on my face? See my eyes? That's what love looks like."

"And you haven't had any relationships since Mom?"

"Not any healthy ones," he said, pausing the video on a close-up of Annie's face. "She was the love of my life."

"But, there *was* someone, after?"

"It doesn't matter."

"Why not?"

"It's complicated."

"I know you're lonely."

Wyatt sighed.

"It looks to me like you miss her, this mystery woman."

"Will,"

"You should call her."

"I shouldn't," Wyatt told him. "The truth is, I do miss her. More than I'd like to admit. But she's not--"

"Interested?"

"Human."

"Oh."

"When you were born, I left the city to keep you safe. I didn't tell her where I was going or even that I was leaving. I ghosted because I knew she'd follow me and you wouldn't have been safe from somebody like her."

"Why no one else, then? A regular person. Why haven't you been on a date in the last three years?"

"I've been kind of busy raising a smart-mouthed son that ages at Mach ten."

"Fair point, but I'm not a baby anymore, Dad. I don't want you to be alone because of me. Call your girlfriend, the whatever-she-is."

"She's a vampire."

"Those are real?! What are they like?"

"Obsessive."

"Is she hot?"

"Shit, yes."

Chapter 13

Wyatt turned off the TV, the remote feeling like failure in his hand. Sleep eluded him, his mind occupied with thoughts of Allydia. Will had been right about him being lonely and as much as it disturbed him to admit, he'd thought about the vampire a lot since leaving the city. She was complicated and a little psychotic, but she wasn't boring, and that alone made the idea of reaching out to her tempting. The last three years hadn't been exactly exciting. Aside from a couple of bouts with a werewolf, life had become unbearably dull. He was used to putting out fires, saving lives...hunting demons. Lately, though, all he seemed to be in life was 'Dad'.

He got up from his chair and headed to the kitchen, deciding he needed a nightcap before trying to get some rest. But, as he took a bottle of beer from the fridge, that eerie feeling once more came over him. He peered out the window, seeing nothing unusual, but the feeling remained. He went out into the backyard, careful to close the door quietly behind him. Will had gone to bed hours ago and he didn't want to wake him. As he walked across the grass, the feeling grew stronger. He knew *something* was out there and had been for a while. The night wrapped around him, the warm, still air of spring like a hug from an old friend. Fireflies danced under the clear sky and the sound of cicadas was the only thing he heard. Maybe he was being paranoid. He was about to turn back when he saw a glimmer among the trees, distinct from anything else in nature. He slowly moved toward it, gathering static electricity from the air in case he needed it. As he drew closer, the shimmering eyes became clearer and as she stepped out from the edge of the forest, he could see that they in fact belonged to Allydia.

"Oh, thank God," he muttered to himself, breaking into a full sprint to meet her. She leaped into his arms, wrapping her legs around him and kissing him fervently. She smelled like gardenias and felt like contentment, her pheromones doing their work to calm and entice him, not that he needed any persuading. He took her to the barn and pressed her to the wall, wasting no time getting his pants down and her skirt up. Her body was like a glove around him, her husky moans like a song. She shuddered against him, the intensity of the moment overwhelming her. He laid her down on the dusty wood floor and continued making love to her, so caught up that he didn't notice the hardness of the ground beneath them. She, too, was oblivious. The only thing she felt was him.

When it was over, he held her face in his hand, watching her eyes as she examined his expression. "Why are you here?" he wondered.

"You know why," she said.

"I missed you."

"Did you?"

"I did."

She ran her fingers down from his forehead to his cheek. "That's nice."

"I'm sorry about taking off like that."

"I understand," she said, turning her head to look toward the house. "And I hope *you* understand why I can't let that boy hurt you." She darted up and out of the barn, running too fast for Wyatt to stop her. He struggled to get his pants on and chase after her at the same time.

"Allydia!" he called. "Wait!" He got to the house to find her standing outside Will's room. He slept soundly, unaware of the threat at his door. "Allydia, stop!" Wyatt whispered.

"What have you done?" she asked.

"It's okay."

"This is a lot of things, Wyatt, but 'okay' is not one of them."

"Come downstairs," he said, taking her hand. She reluctantly followed.

"Do you have any idea what he is?"

"He's fine. He's a good kid."

"He's 'fine'? The last time things like that roamed the planet, your sister had to move me to Spain because your Father destroyed an entire continent to get rid of them."

"Gabriel saved you from the Flood? I didn't know that."

"How else would I still be here? Listen to me, you have no idea what he's capable of. You're not safe here. Come home with me and tell your brother. Let Lucifer handle this before it's too late."

"*Do not* tell Lucifer about Will."

"Wyatt,"

"I mean it."

"I don't appreciate your tone."

"Allydia, he's *my son*. I will *kill* Lucifer before I let him anywhere near--"

"Fine," she said, memories long buried creeping into her mind. Realizing that he'd never forgive her if she was the reason he lost his son, she agreed to back off. "But, if he hurts you, I will take him by the throat and drown him in your bathtub myself."

For the next few nights, Wyatt snuck Allydia up to his room after Will had gone to bed. It was like being in high school again, which somehow made the trysts even more exciting. When she went back to the city, Wyatt couldn't help but miss her. He'd grown fond of having her around; knowing she was keeping an eye on him from the woods was oddly comforting. Twisted and completely unhealthy, but comforting all the same.

Chapter 14

"Close your eyes," Will said, leading Michelle through the woods.

"You know this is how horror movies start, right?" she joked.

"Relax," he chuckled. "Just a few more steps." They finally reached their destination and stopped. "Open your eyes."

She gasped, the beauty of what he'd created surprising her. Twinkling lights wrapped around the trees. A dozen paper lanterns hung overhead, dangling from the branches. Solar-powered lights stuck up out of the ground, encircling an air mattress covered in a blanket. A picnic basket rested on one side of the mattress, the babbling creek on the other. They sat down, Michelle still looking up at the lights.

"Jesus, you're beautiful," he told her, noticing the way the soft light of the lanterns and the early evening sun made her skin glow and her eyes sparkle. She smiled widely and touched his hand and that's when he saw it; the same look that was in his father's eyes in the wedding video was in hers now. She loved him, too. His nerves disappeared as he held her hand, her touch soothing. "I brought you here and I put this together because I want to tell you something. Something important, and I wanted it to be perfect."

"Will," she grinned. "You didn't have to go to all this trouble."

"I did because you deserve it. You deserve more than I could probably ever give you. You're unbelievable and wonderful and I don't know if it's normal to feel like this this soon, and if you can't say it back, I'll understand, but it won't change how I feel about you. Michelle, I am completely, utterly, hopelessly, out of my mind in love with you. It's okay if--"

"I love you, too, Will," she said, squeezing his hand.

"Oh, good. That could've really sucked."

She laughed before kissing him, climbing on top of him, and pushing him to the bed.

"Are we--" he asked. "I mean, do you want to--"

"Do you not want to?" she asked, pulling her top off over her head.

"Oh, I *always* want to, I just didn't want to presume."

"I mean, you *did* bring a picnic. We could eat first if you want."

"No, no, we can eat after. It's not a problem."

"Good," she smirked, unhooking her bra.

As she bent down to kiss him again, he wondered out loud, "Good God, how did I get this lucky?"

He held her as she slept, her head resting comfortably on his chest. He kissed the top of her head through piles of soft curls, the sweet smell of her hair enveloping his senses. He looked up at the starry sky and took a deep breath, happiness blowing through him like wind. It had been a perfect night, one that he knew he'd remember for the rest of his life.

Somewhere in the distance, he heard the rustling of leaves. He lifted his head and looked around, but didn't see anything. Then, on the other side of the creek, as if from thin air, it appeared. Will's eyes became slits as he stared at the wolf, all but daring it to come closer. He held Michelle tighter, continuing to stare down the animal on the other side of the water. The wolf turned away and moved on, vanishing into the dark woods.

"Wake up," Will whispered.

"What?" Michelle asked groggily. "Did I fall asleep?"

"Yeah. It's late. We should go."

She nodded and started putting her clothes back on. They finished dressing and Michelle began deflating the mattress.

"I'll come back in the morning and pack this all up," Will told her. "The lanterns have all gone out. It's pretty dark and there could be wild animals. Let's just go."

"Okay," she agreed, still half asleep. She picked up the picnic basket. "I'm taking this, though. You need to eat."

Michelle woke up the next day to a string of lecture texts from Gabriel.

I didn't think I had to tell you not to date my nephew. You know what he is.

Also, you're almost related. Not really, but still.

Do you have a hormone imbalance that makes you want to hop on the first dick you see or are you just dumb as shit?

That might have been out of line, but I stand by it. I sent you strictly to monitor and report back if he got out of control. THAT'S IT. Fuck!

Try not to die.

Michelle rolled her eyes and set the phone back on the nightstand, pulling her comforter up to her chin, her mind swirling with memories of the night before. The lights, the soft sound of the creek, the warm night air, and Will. Thoughtful, gentle, loving Will. He was sweet and charming and handsome and he loved her. *He loved her.* When he looked at her, she could feel it all through her body, making it that much easier for her to let herself love him, too. She hadn't planned on falling for him so hard, but here she was, aching to see him again.

She picked up the phone to call him, but quickly remembered that he was driving with his father today. She remembered when her uncle had taught her to drive, his hysterical stomping on the nonexistent brake as he sat in the passenger seat of his sports car, clinging to the door handle with one hand and covering his eyes half the time with the other. He eventually sent her to driver's ed classes, telling her he didn't have the disposition to put his life in someone else's hands. She missed Tae every day, but meeting Gabriel had helped her deal with the loss immensely. She'd told her stories about his college days and explained what Heaven was like. Michelle knew her uncle was all right where he was and she'd see him again, someday, along with her parents and grandparents. She was grateful for Gabriel, even if she was wrong about Will. He'd shown no signs of psychopathy, sociopathy, or rage. She'd never seen him use his abilities, much less lose control of them. Gabriel trained her to be able to defend herself in case he ever went crazy, but she was sure Will was no threat to her. He was a good person and he was in love with her. *I'll be fine*, she texted Gabriel back. *Will is okay.*

Chapter 15

Researching humanity's evolution had left Abaddon profoundly disappointed. History was littered with genocide, torture, and war. Every time they seemed to be making progress, people would revert even further into cruelty and narcissism. God had sworn never to rid the Earth of them again, but he'd made no such promise. If his Father would not do what needed to be done, he would simply have to do it himself.

He sat on a park bench, watching the children play. These were the human race's only hope; innocent and gracious. The bit of God in them still shown and as he looked on, he considered the possibility that maybe humanity could be saved after all. Maybe all that was required was a reeducation. When he thought about it, nearly everything a human was was learned behavior. If he could isolate the children, teach them kindness, compassion and selflessness, perhaps the next generation would grow into the people God had always told him they could be. He'd need at least a hundred children to begin the experiment; enough to repopulate if he indeed needed to rid the world of the rest of humanity. He'd need a place to shelter them, as well. There was a cave in Vietnam that could work. It had fresh water and plenty of plant life. He was sure he could grow food there and--

A boy, no more than seven years old, pushed another off a swing, causing Abaddon to lose his train of thought. The second boy cried while the first took his spot on the swing, smiling.

"Or, never mind," Abaddon said to himself, realizing that even the children were tainted. There was no saving these people. He would simply have to remove them like a cancer, forcing his Father to start over, better guiding a new crop of sentient beings, instead of allowing their more animalistic impulses to influence so much of their decision-making.

The second boy ran to his mother, who offered him no comfort as she was preoccupied with the electronic device in her hands. Abaddon wasn't sure if she even knew he was standing there until he saw her reach in her bag and pull out a juice box, handing it to the child without ever taking her eyes off of the screen.

"Shameful," Abaddon groused. He looked back to the first boy who swung gleefully, giving no regard for how he'd made the other boy feel. The disgraced angel became enraged. He reached into his suit jacket pocket and took out a hantavirus carrying rat. He whispered something into its tiny ear and released it on the ground in front of him. The rodent scurried toward the swinging boy, but before it could reach his shoe, its neck inexplicably snapped, its head spinning around one hundred and eighty degrees. The boy screamed and ran off, allowing the crying boy to retake his rightful place on the contraption. Abaddon scanned the area but saw no one who could perform such a trick. Lucifer was nowhere in sight and while he was aware of the demons that escaped Hell along with him, none of them had telekinetic powers. Someone else must be on Earth. Someone powerful. He stood and left the park, not wanting to risk a run-in with whoever was following him.

Gabriel got home from the park and read Michelle's reply, *Will is okay.* "You better be right, bitch," she said under her breath.

"I'd better what?" Lucifer asked.

"Not you."

"Right, well, the polio outbreak in Myanmar proved to be caused by a lack of vaccine, not Abaddon."

"Back to square one, then?"

"Unfortunately," Lucifer said. "Would you mind ordering lunch? I'm feeling rather peckish and the only food you keep here is artificially flavored."

Gabriel ignored his comment and opened the laptop to order food. Lucifer hovered behind her, groaning in disapproval when she chose two servings of mashed potatoes for herself. She let out a sigh of derision before slamming the computer closed and asking him, "Why are you like this?"

Chapter 16

"So," Malik said. "You ready to move in with your husband?"

"Mm, 'husband'," Valerie said, her lips curling into a smile. "I like the way that sounds." She kissed him hard as the cab drove on, the Manhattan traffic moving slower than the Venetian gondola rides she'd gotten used to. The past week had been a feast of food and sex, occasionally at the same time. She was still surprised that she had Lucifer to thank for setting it all up. Maybe he wasn't so terrible, after all.

The cab stopped, jolting the couple from their newly-wedded bliss. They had been so distracted, they hadn't noticed that the driver had pulled into an alley and was now quietly laughing.

"Why'd you stop?" Malik snapped.

"Ask your friend," the cabbie hissed, still giggling.

"Oh, shit," Valerie gulped, realizing what he was. She could see through the mirror his ashen skin and sunken cheeks; his bloodshot eyes and teeth half-missing.

"Hey, man," Malik started, but Valerie cut him off.

"Get out," she told him.

"What?"

"Get out the cab! Get the fuck out!" she ordered, pushing him to the door, but it was too late. The demon threw itself into the back seat and began clawing at them like a rabid animal. Marks appeared on Malik's face, blood dripping from them to his shirt which the demon clutched in his veiny hand. Valerie opened her door and squeezed out, the alley barely wide enough for the cab to fit. She reached through the driver's side window and took the keys from the ignition. She opened the trunk and rifled through her husband's bag. "Kick its ass, baby!" she called, hoping Malik could hold his own until she got back. Finally, she found what she was looking for. She took the biggest knife from her husband's chef knife set and watched as it burst into flames. She ran to Malik's door and yanked the demon out of the cab by his hair. She stabbed it repeatedly until fire spread over its entire body, its screams deafening as it fell to the ground. She dropped the blade and helped Malik from the car, looking him over for wounds.

"Are you okay?" she fretted, seeing the many scratches and bite marks that covered his face and arms.

"What the hell was that, Val?!" he asked, more like an accusation than a question.

"Don't yell at me."

"Valerie, what the fu--"

"It was a demon."

"A *what*?"

"I should probably tell you something."

Lucifer prowled the streets for hours, but no demons could be found. It was odd because he knew there were thousands of them on the loose and he'd assumed at least some of them would have stayed in the city. The high concentration of people made it hard to resist. Since demons didn't bother tending to their hosts, body-hopping was necessary if they wanted to stay on Earth for more than a month or so. Manhattan should have been crawling with the fiends. They were up to something.

As he passed an alleyway, he felt a familiar sensation. The hair on the back of his neck stood up and he felt slightly nauseated. He walked toward a cab parked precariously in the alley, a satisfied smirk crossing his lips as he bent down to inspect the body that lay next to it, the corpse burned nearly to ash.

Seeing the puncture marks on what was left of the torso, he laughed, "Welcome home, Uriel."

He was bored; with no demons to exorcise and no idea where Abaddon was, he grew increasingly impatient, restless, and angry. He knew it wouldn't be long before he did something he'd no doubt get a lecture from Gabriel for. Perhaps his sister was right. Yes, Mariana was a distraction, and yes, he would be shirking his duties by taking time to meet with her. But, he needed to blow off some steam, and spending time with a beautiful woman was less regrettable than mass murder. Usually.

He called the number she'd given him years earlier, hoping it still worked. It did.

"Hello?" she answered.

"Mariana, hello. I don't know if you remember me, but-"

"Lou?"

"Yes. You recognized my voice?"

"Of course. I think about that day *a lot*."

"Well, that's lovely to hear. I'm recently back in town and I was wondering--"

"I'll text you my address."

Lucifer opened the door to the five-story walk-up, checking the mailboxes to make sure he was in the right place. Behind the first set of stairs, a teenaged boy threw lit firecrackers at a stray cat. The feline hissed and backed away, but the boy had it trapped in a milk crate fortress. *Obnoxious little prick,* Lucifer thought. He made a gesture toward them, giving the cat the courage to defend itself. It leaped at the boy, clawing at his face and eyes. The boy screamed and tried to run, tripping over himself and falling on his behind. The cat kept coming, mauling his face into a bloody mess. Lucifer snickered as he made his way up to the third floor. He got to apartment 3C and lifted his hand to knock, but before his knuckles met the door, it flew open, Mariana having been watching through the peephole for the past few minutes in anticipation of his arrival.

"Hey," she purred.

"Mariana," he said. "You're looking ravishing as ever. Might I--"

"Get in here," she ordered, grabbing him by the shirt and pulling him in, kissing him with three years of unrequited passion. Lucifer was delightfully surprised, wrapping his arms around her waist and kicking the door closed behind him thinking, *Wouldn't want the moment to be ruined by the screams of a psychotic juvenile.*

Chapter 17

Valerie walked into Gabriel's apartment without knocking and sat silently on a stool at the bar. She looked tired and had obviously been crying.

"You want me to hurt him a little?" Gabriel asked, getting her sister a soda from the fridge.

"No, girl. I just didn't want to go back to my apartment. It's too quiet."

"What's happened, sister?" Lucifer asked, joining the women in the kitchen. "Married life not all it's cracked up to be?"

"Not now, Satan."

"I am not-"

"Yo, Daddy's favorite," Gabriel warned. "She said not now."

"Are you jealous?" Lucifer poked.

"Nah, I got cooler powers."

"Did you? Tell me then, when was the last time *you* flew?"

"When was the last time *you* set something on fire with your brain?"

"I know I said my place was too quiet," Valerie told them. "But do you two ever shut the fuck up?"

"Look at me," Gabriel said, sitting across from her at the island. "Are you looking?"

"You see I am," Valerie sighed.

"Malik will come back when the shock wears off. He will. It's just gonna take a minute for his tiny human brain to wrap itself around all this new information. It's not every day you find out your wife's an angel, like, literally. His face when you told him about Lucifer," she giggled, having seen how the conversation had played out as soon as Valerie walked in. "I'll be laughing about that for *days*." Valerie shot her an annoyed squint. "Sorry."

"Was he scared?" Lucifer asked.

"Shitless," Gabriel confirmed.

"Really?"

"Figuratively."

"Well, that's mildly disappointing."

"I just," Valerie croaked. "I just wanted this so bad. Something normal. Husband, kids, maybe a fuckin' dog. A regular, safe, stable life. After all the bullshit growing up, I thought I deserved something better. He was my chance."

"He'll come back," Gabriel said. "And, if he doesn't--"

"If he doesn't, I'll kill him," Lucifer promised.

"No," Gabriel said.

"I can make it painless if you prefer, though that takes all the fun out of it."

"*No.*"

"Why ever not? He's hurt our sister. That alone demands retribution. Not to mention the fact that *he knows what we are*. Humans can't handle that kind of knowledge, as well you know. Wars have been fought over it. People go mad. We can't allow this to get out. Not while Father slumbers. If he tells anyone--"

"He won't," Valerie assured him.

"But, if he does--"

Valerie gasped, her eyes opening wide.

"Are you all right?" Lucifer asked.

"She's having a vision," Gabriel explained. "I haven't been here for one of these in years." She grabbed a bag of chips and eagerly watched what was happening in Valerie's mind while Lucifer placed a hand on her temple so he, too, could enjoy the show.

The silent street was littered with bodies, the air heavy with the stench of death. Broadway had never been this quiet. Valerie stepped over the corpses, mutilated and disfigured, some looking as though they'd rotted from the inside out. She realized those must have been the hosts for long-gone demons while the rest were innocent people, caught in the crosshairs of evil. She came upon a newspaper box and took note of the date, only three days away. She then heard the unmistakable sound of a demon screeching in the distance. As it got louder, she could tell that it wasn't just one voice, but several. The closer it became, the more voices she could make out. There were dozens, then hundreds, then thousands. It was so loud, it vibrated the glass on the surrounding buildings. Electric billboards shook and exploded. Car alarms sounded as the ground beneath her trembled. This wasn't the sound of a few escaped Fallen. This was Hell itself. Every damned soul, every once imprisoned monster now laid claim to the Earth, extinguishing humanity from it like a twisted exterminator. Nowhere was safe. The world was theirs.

Valerie shivered as she came reeling out of the vision, terror replacing the sadness she'd felt just moments before. Gabriel went to the pantry and pulled the small box from behind the cereal, tossing it to Lucifer and giving him a knowing stare. He opened it, looking pensively at the amulet inside and back at his sister.

"You don't have a choice," she told him.

"I don't know that our Father would see it that way."

"When I get up there, I'll explain it to Him. Right now, though,"

"Yes," he agreed. "You're right, as always." He lifted his shirt and took a deep breath, plucking the amulet from the box and plunging it into his chest, grunting as the stone sank beneath the muscle and rested just over his heart.

"What the fuck?!" Valerie yelped, jumping up from her seat.

"I'll be back," he told them, turning toward the balcony and wiping the blood on his pants.

"Where you goin'?"

Lucifer opened the French doors, grateful night had fallen, the chances of someone seeing him fly overhead lessened. "Yonkers."

Locals called this abandoned power station "The Gate to Hell". They didn't know how right they were. Underneath the graffiti, broken bricks, and barred windows lie something darker than the water outside under the moonless sky. The vortex, not visible to the human eye, stood open and unguarded, leaving anything to get out that had the courage to try. Few demons on the streets meant that they were gathering somewhere, plotting. Lilith was under lock and key, he'd made sure of it, but others, no doubt, had taken up her mantle. Hell on Earth had been the pipe dream of every demon since their imprisonment. With Lucifer gone and the Gate wide open, this was their chance to make that fantasy a reality.

Though it pained him, he waved his hand over the mass of dark, watching as it drew in on itself. The shrieks of the damned were so loud and high pitched, it made his ears bleed. Thousands of screaming shadows poured into the building, fighting futilely against the pull of the murky whirlwind. The vortex closed, every demon back where it belonged, the Gate locked tight. Lucifer dropped to his knees, the guilt of what he'd done, what he had to do, like a weight on his spirit. There was no way of going back for him until his Father woke and there would be no exorcising Abaddon now. Death was the only option.

He again lifted his shirt and tore the amulet from his chest, howling in pain as blood seeped from the wound. While he healed, he looked over the stone, Chinese engravings and beautiful embellishments covering its face. Gabriel had known this would happen; that it would *have* to happen. She was prepared. "What else are you hiding from me, sister?" he muttered. He shoved the rock in his pocket and walked out to the edge of the river. He cleaned himself up and looked back at the building. He couldn't shake the guilt, knowing it was against God's Law for him to remain on Earth as long as he'd now have to. The feeling was unpleasant, so he decided to replace it with another. He took his phone from his back pocket and called Mariana.

"Hello, love," he said when she answered. "I realize it's late and we've just seen each other, but, would you perhaps be up for another round?"

Chapter 18

"Just aim for the pins," Michelle said.

"I know the rules of bowling," Will told her. "I've just never actually played before."

"Okay, but you've been standing there for three and a half minutes staring at the lane like you don't know how to roll a ball, so."

"I'm going," he said, stepping forward and releasing the ball down the smooth wood floor. The pins sounded like thunder as they flew and fell to their sides.

"Strike!" Michelle yelped, standing from her seat in the booth to give her boyfriend a quick peck on the cheek. "Good job, sweetie."

"See? I just had to take my time."

"Oh, okay," she teased, taking her ball and waiting for the pins to reset. As she stood there, she noticed a middle-aged man in a torn tee-shirt and faded jeans two lanes over watching her. His unkempt dirty-blond hair fell over one eye, sticking out from his backward blue baseball cap. *Well, he's creepy,* she thought. She rolled her ball down the lane; a seven-ten split.

"You got this, M!" Will called from the booth. When the bar raised, she took her shot. She threw the ball hard toward the pin on the left, sending it careening across to the other side. The pins collided, both of them falling. "Holy crap!" Will exclaimed. He picked her up and swung her around, kissing her before setting her back on her feet. "Where did you learn to bowl like that?"

"My uncle used to take me. Once a month, we'd go blacklight bowling. He said it was the only sport he was good at, but I think he just went to pick up dudes."

Will laughed. "Well, I'm glad he took you because you are an amazing teacher." He kissed her again before taking his ball and stepping forward. She tried to ignore it, but she could feel the man in the other lane still staring.

She could see him from the corner of her eye, facing her, not even attempting to be subtle. She made the mistake of letting her eyes wander in his direction and regretted it immediately. The man held up two fingers, pointed at his own eyes, and then to her. It felt like a threat of some kind and she grew increasingly uncomfortable; so much so that she didn't see Will's second strike of the night.

"Are you all right?" Will asked, seeing the distress on her face.

"Can we go?" she asked quietly.

"What do you mean? We just started."

"I don't want to be here. I want to go. Can we go?"

She looked nervous, downright afraid. "Yeah," he said, putting his ball down. "Yeah, let's go." They changed their shoes and headed for the door as the man continued to watch. Michelle put Will's arm around her as they reached the parking lot and walked toward her car.

Just a few more steps, she thought.

"For future reference," Will said. "If you ever want to leave a place, you don't need to ask. Just tell me we're leaving. I'll go wherever you want me to."

"Thanks, sweetie."

"Isn't that precious?" the man from inside scoffed, running in front of them, blocking their path. "Where do you think you're going?" he asked the couple, the smell of stale beer and cheap cigarettes wafting off of him.

"Excuse us," Michelle said politely, hoping to avoid an altercation.

"Maybe you didn't hear me," he said, his voice raised. "I asked where the hell you think you're going."

"What's your problem, man?" Will demanded.

"I wasn't talking to you, bitch," the man dismissed, pushing Will to the ground. He grabbed Michelle's arm and pulled her close to him. "You're not going anywhere."

She struggled to free herself and before she could whip out her best Krav Maga moves, Will was on top of him.

He threw the man to the ground, sitting on his chest and hitting him repeatedly, breaking his nose and jaw. He could feel himself losing control, but he didn't care. No one hurt Michelle. *No one.* He hit the man again, breaking his left eye socket, and again, knocking out a few teeth. With his final punch, his fist sparked with electricity. On impact, the man began to shake as if he were having a seizure. It was then that he realized what he'd done and could finally hear Michelle's screams.

"I'm sorry," he said, standing, his hands trembling. The man's face was unrecognizable. Will feared the worst, but as the bully lay there twitching, he could hear him groan in pain. He was alive.

"We have to go," Michelle said, grabbing Will by the shirt. "Come on!" She looked around to make sure no one saw what had happened and got in the car. Once Will was in, she sped off, concern growing in her like fungus. "What the hell was that, Will?"

"He was hurting you. I just...snapped."

"You can't lose control like that. I know he was a dick, but--"

"He was *hurting you.* I don't know if he's racist or if that was like a 'me too' thing, but I had to protect you. I *had* to."

"Why, because you're the guy?" she condescended.

"No, because you're important," he told her. "I love you. If someone grabbed *me* like that, what would *you* have done?"

"Fine, but you're lucky that guy's not dead," she lectured, turning onto Will's street. "It could've been really bad. You know that, right? You understand what could've happened, right?"

"I know."

"You hit him really hard."

"Yeah," he said, thankful she hadn't seen the electrocution. "*Really* hard."

"I'm not fragile. I can take care of myself."

"I know you can. I wasn't trying to--"

"And I don't want you thinking you have to swoop in and rescue me all the time. If you'd given me a few seconds, I would've handed that guy his ass myself." She parked in the driveway and turned off the engine. "I appreciate that you care about me. I do. But, I don't need you to be my knight in shining armor. I don't need a bodyguard. What I *need* is for you to stay as sweet and kind as you've always been. I don't want anything bad to happen to you."

"Okay," he told her. "I promise, from now on, no more saving the day."

"Thank you. Now, go ice that hand before it swells." She kissed him softly and watched as he made his way to the door and inside the house. She looked down at her phone, debating whether or not to tell Gabriel of the night's events. She knew he just did what any boyfriend would have in that situation, but his strength was far greater than that of a regular guy's. The raw power with which he beat that man bloody, while sexy, was dangerous, and the burst of electricity from his hand troubled her. Gabriel had told her what he was capable of, but she hadn't quite believed it. She'd never seen anything like it.

"This is why she said not to get too close," she said to herself, remembering the speeches about keeping a safe distance, staying an acquaintance, nothing more, and watching from afar. She wasn't sure if her feelings for him were clouding her judgement or if the incident really wasn't that big of a deal. She put her phone down and started the car, deciding not to involve Gabriel. One outburst of violence in defense of the person he loves didn't constitute a flag red enough that he deserved to die. She would keep watching, waiting, and hoping that everything would be all right.

Will went straight through the house, closing the front door behind him and heading out the back. He hadn't wanted to scare Michelle, so he had feigned calm in the car, but he was *not* calm. He was angry to the point of rage, still seeing the man's hand on his girlfriend's arm, manhandling her with such entitlement, as if she were his property. He needed to vent, to rid himself of this negative energy. Though the man in the parking lot may have deserved an ass-kicking, Will had scared himself with the electrical discharge. He hadn't meant to do it and a loss of control like that *couldn't* happen again. He decided to go into the woods where his father had set up a few rubber targets. They'd been practicing aim, restraint, and authority over his ability, and if the night's events proved one thing, it was that he was *not* in full control. He needed *a lot* more training.

He threw one ball of lightning after another, telling himself to constrain them to no more powerful than a car battery. But, as he continued, his rage only grew stronger, and so did his blasts. He launched another and another, their size and power increasing with every throw. He pulled his arm back like a pitcher in a baseball game and released a surge of lightning so forceful that the tree the target was strapped to snapped and fell backward, crashing loudly to the ground. He was stunned, never having wielded that much power before. He was sure the noise had woken his father, so he turned to exit the forest. In the distance, he could hear a wolf howl. His anger not yet dissipated, he changed his mind and headed back.

"Will?" Wyatt called from upstairs.

"Yeah, Dad, I'm just getting a snack!" Will called back, having finished two sandwiches already. He took some pain reliever and started on sandwich number three.

"You ready for your next driving lesson tomorrow?" Wyatt asked as he came down the stairs.

"Yeah, it'll be nice being able to pick Michelle up for a date instead of the other way around all the time. Hey, Dad,"

"Yeah?"

Will paused. He knew he should tell his father what had happened. It was rule number one. If he ever lost control or scared himself, he was supposed to tell. But, he was afraid. He didn't want his dad to think of him differently or lock him up somewhere. "I, um, I smashed my hand in the car door," he lied, showing Wyatt his banged-up knuckles.

"Oh, man!" Wyatt said, inspecting Will's fist. "Let's get some ice on that. What happened?"

"I just got distracted. Michelle was--"

"Say no more," Wyatt chuckled, wrapping a bag of frozen peas in a paper towel and handing it to his son. "You able to drive? Hold the steering wheel properly?"

"I'm pretty sure, yeah," Will told him, amazed he hadn't mentioned the tree falling. He hadn't heard. Since Valerie cleaned up his subconscious, he slept fairly heavily. His alarm barely woke him. He had to have it set to ring continuously until it was manually turned off, just in case. After years of torment, his mind now rested soundly, making up for lost time.

"I was planning on waiting until you got your license, but,"

"But what?" Will asked, unable to hide his excitement.

"Look in the garage."

"You didn't," Will said, running to the door and swinging it open into the three-car garage. There, next to his father's car, was another. Its gunmetal paint shined under the dim overhead light, its smooth curves reminding him of a toy he played with as a child. "You did! That's for me, right? Dad, I love it!"

"I thought you might," Wyatt grinned, accepting the hug his son gave him.

"And I can take it out tomorrow?"

"Sure, just be careful. I don't want to have to pay to fix a car I just bought."

"I'll take care of it, I promise. Michelle's gonna love it."

"Kid, if she was the kind of girl that got impressed by the kind of car a guy has, she wouldn't be dating someone that can't drive."

"Yeah, she's awesome."

"So, things are going well?"

"Yeah, she's the best," Will gushed.

"Good, that's nice for you. And, who knows? Maybe your old man's not out of the game, after all."

"The vampire?!"

Wyatt shrugged coyly and went back inside.

"Dad," Will pried, following him. "Come on, Dad! I need details!"

Chapter 19

Lucifer slept comfortably in Mariana's bed for the second night in a row. He would never tell her, but Gabriel had been right about him needing to take a break. He felt recharged, ready to take on Abaddon, wherever he may be. He'd get back to the search in the morning, after one more go-round with the beauty sleeping beside him. As he fell deeper into his slumber, he began to dream, first of Mariana and then of home. Not Hell; his *real* home. He dreamed of his brother, Michael, telling him that he was doing exactly what he was meant to and that their Father was pleased with him. He could feel the warmth of Heaven, the complete, unconditional love of every soul there. He could hear the distant hum of God's voice and as he turned to look, thrilled by the promise of seeing his Father's face after so many millennia, the scene changed. Now, he stood in a cheap motel room, a burnt orange blanket on the bed, pea soup green shag carpet covering the floor.

"What is this?" he griped, lucid and resentful.

"It's no Perdition," Abaddon quipped. "But it's been home."

"You repugnant, loathsome--"

"Now, now, don't be cross. I come in peace, as they say."

"I will pull your lungs from your body and watch with glee as you suffocate."

"I will ignore that, seeing as how I interrupted your homecoming fantasy. Your vexation is understandable. I, too, have wished, in vain, to go back to Heaven. But we will never be welcomed back through the Gates, as you well know."

"*You* won't. But, *I--*"

"You were condemned to Hell in service to our Father for infinity. You will never go home. When the scourge of humanity is scrubbed clean from this world, God will only create another race of pets he can fawn over that will no doubt need protecting. You will forever be charged with keeping the demons at bay, unless you give up your mantle, and join me."

"*Join you?*" Lucifer scoffed. "I mean to *kill you*."

"Come now, brother. Try to remember Earth as it was before the human curse. Tranquil and serene. Clean. It could be again."

"And when God wakes? I don't think you've thought this through. Besides, what's the point of being on Earth if you can't enjoy humanity? There are benefits to these bodies that you've clearly failed to explore."

"You're more brutish than I remember," Abaddon complained.

"And you're more deluded."

"Have it your way, but I won't spare you when I end this ridiculous experiment."

"And how do you plan on doing that? People aren't as helpless as they once were. They've developed medicines. You'll have a difficult time plaguing them all."

"I've discovered something called 'internet'," Abaddon explained. "Have you heard of it? I have access to all the world's knowledge on a device called 'computer'."

"Yes, I'm familiar."

"The one thing humanity seems to be unrelentingly skilled at is the development of weapons of war. I will use their own wickedness against them and wipe them clean from the Earth, once and for all."

"You will regret--"

"My only regret will be that they'll die too swiftly to recognize the evil in their own hearts."

Lucifer woke abruptly, springing to a sitting position and startling Mariana.

"Are you okay?" she asked, half-asleep.

"Fine, love," he told her, catching his breath. "Go back to sleep. I'm off. I'll call you later. I have work to do."

Lucifer stood outside the motel, contemplating exactly how he'd make his presence known. He'd recognized the interior of the building from the last time he'd been on Earth, having tracked a demon nest there when he went searching for Lilith. Abaddon had been so smug, thinking he could hide from him forever. He would soon find out how wrong he was.

Lucifer made a turning motion with his left hand, raising it to the sky, his eyes fixed on the building in front of him. The clouds above began to swirl, the gentle spring breeze growing in speed. The skies darkened as a funnel cloud formed, the wind pushing cars around the parking lot like toys. The roof of the building peeled away, leaving screaming residents to scramble to lower ground. All but one. Abaddon looked through the now broken window of his room, shocked that he'd been found. Lucifer sneered back, bringing his arm, and the tornado, down, ripping through the building and sending Abaddon flying into a car just a few feet from where Lucifer stood, a smirk on his face and delight in his eyes.

"You should have stayed hidden," he said, allowing the skies to calm and the weather to return to normal.

"You will not stop me," Abaddon told him, getting to his feet, blood trickling from his mouth. He lifted the car and hurled it at Lucifer, who stepped slightly to his right, avoiding an impact and rolling his eyes.

"You'll have to do better than that. Remember who I am."

"Yes," Abaddon mocked. "God's favorite son. The most beautiful angel in all of Heaven."

"Yes, that, but more importantly," he picked up a truck and hit him, swinging it like a baseball bat, sending him hurling into what was left of the building. "The strongest."

Abaddon struggled to stand, blood pouring from his mouth and nose. He held his ribs, the broken bones taking more time than he'd like to heal. He coughed, unable to get his balance. "Was it you, then?" he accused. "In the park? Like a sick game of cat and mouse, biding your time, letting me think I was safe?"

"I haven't been to a park in ages," Lucifer said. "Must have been Gabriel. What'd she do? Move you against your will? Set you on fire? She does have an affinity for pyrotechnics."

"Gabriel? How is *she* here?"

"You know our Father, all-knowing and such. He saw you and Lilith coming and sent some of our more agile siblings as a means of defense." Lucifer retrieved a downed lamppost, hoisting it over his shoulder. "We put Lilith back in a cage, which was the fate I'd intended for you. But, sadly, the demon hordes got antsy waiting for my return, so they came forth, overrunning this planet and planning an Apocalypse. I had to send them back from whence they came by locking the Gate."

"You didn't. You would never disobey so blatantly. Too afraid of God's wrath."

"I did what I had to. So, no way back in for us, and since I can't allow you to destroy the human race, well, you see where that leaves me."

"You can't kill me," Abaddon dismissed. "I'm immortal."

"Did I not mention the presence of our dear sister? Her Holy Fire can eradicate even your true form. You won't die, per se. You'll simply cease to exist."

"Where is she?" Abaddon shouted, Lucifer relishing the hint of anxiety in his voice.

"Oh, who knows. Her schedule of errands and meetings with this or that lover is impossible to predict. However, I can summon her here with a thought, and I will, once I've had my fun." He swung the post back and brought it forward, but before it could make contact, Abaddon was gone, teleporting off to who knows where. Rage replaced glee as Lucifer dropped the post, a scowl covering his once contented expression. He growled under his breath, his fists and jaw clenched. He knew now what Abaddon was planning, it was simply a matter of location. He flew off, knowing he didn't have much time to narrow it down.

Chapter 20

Abaddon materialized in the Sonoran desert, not far from Mobile, Arizona. He walked for miles, having no idea what direction led to where, deciding that a place this desolate was perfect for hiding from Lucifer for a time. He was tired and hungry, the body he'd chosen never relenting in its petty weaknesses. His ribs were still not fully healed and the pain was getting to be more and more of a nuisance as he wandered, the heat making him reconsider the jacket he wore. He went to unbutton it, but his fingers didn't cooperate. The sun beat down on him with such unyielding warmth that he, in his current condition, could not withstand it. His knees buckled and as he fell to the scorched earth below, his blurred vision went dark. By the time his head hit the ground, he could feel nothing, all of his senses having left him, floating away into the arid afternoon air.

Abaddon woke with a start, the vibrations underneath him foreign and unpleasant. He was seated inside of a truck, not unlike the one Lucifer had struck him with. He was unamused by the irony.

"You okay, buddy?" the man in the driver's seat asked, reaching for a bottle of water from the cup holder and handing it to him. He was older, probably in his sixties or so, with eyes as blue as the pattern on his flannel shirt. "You need a doctor? Want me to call someone for you?"

"No, thank you," Abaddon replied. "I'm fine." He sipped the water, annoyed by how delicious it tasted, maddened by his need for a human host, to begin with. Everything about a physical body was aggravating and tedious. He took no pleasure in occupying one and was sickened by his unwilling relief as the water soothed his throat and cooled his internal temperature.

"I found you face-planted a few miles back. You are not 'fine'. Blood on your face, no wallet or phone. Looks like you got robbed."

"I wasn't, I assure you. Thank you for the water. You can let me out anywhere."

"Buddy, I don't know how they do things where you're from, but around here, if someone needs help, which you *clearly* do, you help them. Now, I can understand not wanting to go to the hospital. Can't stand the places myself. But, I'd be a grade-A piece of shit if I didn't at least give you somewhere to clean up. You hungry? I'm grilling burgers for dinner. You're more than welcome."

"That's very compassionate of you," Abaddon said, surprised by the stranger's generosity.

"No problem. And you don't have to tell me what happened to you out there. None of my business."

"You wouldn't believe me."

"Don't go piquing my interest," the old man snickered, reaching over to shake his passenger's hand. "Name's Ed, Ed Stone."

Abaddon shook the man's hand, having seen the custom dozens of times on television. "Abaddon."

The man laughed. "You are foreign, ain't ya? What kind of name is that? Greek?"

"Hebrew."

"Huh. Well, it's definitely interesting. You Jewish, then? Lot's of Jews out this way. I'm Baptist, myself, but, to each their own."

"I don't participate in the mass delusion of organized religion, no offense."

"None taken. Everyone's entitled to their own beliefs. The love of my life was Muslim. I don't judge." They pulled into the driveway of a small suburban home, Abaddon taking note of how similar all of the houses on the street looked. They exited the red pickup and headed to the door, Ed unlocking it and inviting his guest inside. "Bathroom's the second door on the left," he offered, pointing down the hall. "You can get cleaned up while I get the burgers on. You want something to drink? I have soda and juice. I don't drink alcohol, so no beer, sorry."

"Water's fine, thank you," Abaddon told him before entering the bathroom. He wet a hand towel and wiped the dried blood from his nose, mouth, and chin. Lucifer had done a number on him, but he couldn't do any permanent damage. He and Gabriel together, however, could very well be a different story. He'd have to avoid them until he regained his strength. Perhaps he should speak to Gabriel, one-on-one. The only way she could be outside Heaven's Gates was if she, too, was tethered to one of these miserable corporeal forms. Maybe he could convince her that ridding the planet of these wretched bodies was in her best interest. She'd be free of the constant torture of putrid bodily fluids and functions, the biological urges and requirements that her true form didn't need. She could shed herself of it and go home, back to Heaven, where she belonged.

He dropped the towel in the hamper behind him and looked back in the mirror, studying the face of the man he inhabited. He wasn't sure what would happen to him once his work was done. If he allowed this body to perish with the rest of humanity, where would he go? Not back to Hell, thanks to Lucifer. Not to Heaven; he was banned, not to mention the spell he'd cast all those millennia ago. He was fixed to the Earth, but without an anchor in the form of a human host, his atoms would scatter. He'd lose his sense of self and become little more than dust in the wind. No. As much as he hated the confinement of this body, he'd have to protect it.

He left the bathroom and gave himself a tour of the house, peeking into rooms, examining the art on the walls, and inspecting the books on the shelf in the living room. Two Bibles, one King James, and one New International version. Books on architecture, bird watching, and entomology. As he looked around, he was confused by the lack of pictures in the home. He'd never actually been inside someone's home before, so it probably wasn't that unusual, but homes on television always had photos in frames sitting on end tables or hanging on walls. Tables here held only golf magazines and coasters and the art on the walls consisted of watercolor paintings of fish, bears, and deer. It was obvious to him that the man must live alone, but what of the 'love of his life' he'd mentioned?

"Burgers are done!" Ed called, opening the sliding glass door that led to the back patio and poking his head in. "Perfect medium-rare." He took the plate of meat to the kitchen and began building burgers, placing lettuce and pickles on the bottom buns and squirting ketchup and mustard on the tops before adding the patties and closing them up. He put a heap of chips on both plates and brought them to the dining table where Abaddon had politely sat. "Bon appetit!"

"Thank you," Abaddon said, eating a chip, angered by how amazing the burgers smelled.

"So, Abaddon, what do you do for a living?"

"Do you mean for money?"

"Well, yeah."

"Money is a man-made construct I don't quite understand. It only has value because someone says it does. I suppose that's true of most things here, but I find it perplexing. What people are willing to do for it and the desperate longing they feel for it. It's obscene."

"You're right about that. 'The love of money is the root of all evil'. Inflation being what it is, young people can't afford to live the way my generation did. Living with their parents until they're thirty, can't afford a house, student loans taking what little income they have. It's not right." The man took a bite of his dinner, nearly choking on it when Abaddon spoke again.

"So, where's your wife?"

"My wife?" Ed sputtered, taking a sip of his soda.

"You mentioned her on the way here."

"Ah, 'the love of my life'." A forlorn stare into the distance replaced the chipper smile on the man's face, heartbreak apparent in his voice. "She left, a little over a year ago."

"I'm sorry. I shouldn't have asked."

"No, it's fine. It's good to talk about her. Remembering the good times makes it less painful."

"What was she like?"

"She was beautiful. Big brown eyes, skin the color of coffee. She wore henna on her hands and a hijab on her head. Her name was Sabita and she was wonderful. I miss her every day."

"It sounds like you loved her very much."

"I still do. I would do anything to bring her back if I could." The men finished eating in silence, melancholy hanging like fog in the air. Evening turned to night, Ed sharing stories of Sabita, his work at the church, and his latest fishing trip to Saguaro Lake. His life was lonely but full and Abaddon felt a strange sense of guilt thinking about how he'd die in a blanket of fire and ash later.

"It's getting late," Ed sighed, his joints cracking as he stood from the sofa. "You look a lot better than you did, but not a hundred percent. There's a guest room down the hall if you'd like to stay the night."

"That would be very helpful, thank you," Abaddon accepted.

"All right, I'm going to bed. This old man can't burn the midnight oil like he used to."

"Goodnight, Ed."

"Goodnight." Ed shuffled off to his room and closed the door, Abaddon following behind to the guest room. He sat on the bed, pondering the generosity and kindness of the man, a stranger to him until today. He'd found him, unconscious and bleeding, and instead of leaving him to die or merely calling the authorities, he'd taken it upon himself to feed and shelter him for the evening for no other reason than it's what he considered to be the right thing to do. Ed was a genuinely decent human being. Had he judged humanity too harshly? How many more people were as honorable as Ed? Was the human race worth sparing? Perhaps instead of a mass execution of the entire species, he could spend some time extracting the good ones from the general population and protecting them from what was to come. It would take time and much more effort, but men like Ed were a beacon of goodness in an otherwise festering cesspool of immorality. More like him could teach future generations what it means to be human, the way God had originally intended. His Father would undoubtedly be miffed that he exterminated most of his favorite pets, but once He saw the utopia Abaddon created, He'd have no choice but to let it stand. Who knows? He might even forgive him.

    He stood, unbuttoning and removing his suit jacket. He opened the closet door and hung it on a hanger. As he placed the hanger back on its rack, he took notice of a jewelry box on the floor in the back left corner of the closet. Curiosity got the better of him and he picked it up. It was a pale shade of pink and played a quiet melody when opened. What he found inside horrified and enraged him.

    At the bottom was a neatly folded pair of girl's panties. Atop that was a lock of hair and pictures of what he recognized from the internet as 'kiddie porn'. Polaroid after Polaroid of children in compromising poses, some in just underwear, some in nothing at all. A stack of photos that had been separated from the others, tied together with a red ribbon, infuriated him more than anything else he'd seen. They were all of the same girl who looked to be ten or eleven years old with dark skin, large, frightened eyes, wearing a hijab. "Love of his life," Abaddon seethed.

    "Hey, buddy," Ed said, opening the door to the guest room, carrying a bottle of water. "Thought you might need--" He stopped, seeing what Abaddon had discovered. "You don't understand."

"You're right," Abaddon agreed, setting the jewelry box and its contents on a shelf in the closet and loosening his tie. "I don't understand. I don't understand how a race that was handed Paradise can destroy it without a second thought. I don't understand how you all abide unjust and corrupt laws designed to make a very few of you even more wealthy. I don't understand murder, genocide, slavery, greed, lying, or hatred. I don't understand the cruelty in which you all seem to relish. And, mostly, at this moment, I don't understand how a creature as vile as *you* could have fooled me into thinking you were worth saving."

"I didn't hurt them," Ed insisted. "I just took pictures."

"And what became of those children after you'd taken your sick pleasure? What became of Sabita?"

"Well," he hesitated. "She told her parents, so,"

"So what, Ed?" Abaddon barked, his rage growing.

"I had to."

"You had to what?!"

"I, I called ICE."

Abaddon's blood boiled. "You're telling me you had a family deported to spare yourself justice?"

"I know, it's bad, but it's not what you think. It's a *disease*."

"A disease," Abaddon rasped. "Funny you should mention." He waved his hand in Ed's direction, a calmness returning to his demeanor. "I don't pretend to know what living with the mind of a pervert is like, but I do know that God gave you all highly functioning brains, capable of self-control and rational thought. You *decide* how you treat others and if you can not, you seek the help of professionals that can teach you, or, if no other recourse can be taken, can lock you away from civilized society."

Ed began to feel a burning sensation in his genitals. It got worse quickly, forcing him to drop his pants and examine himself right there in front of his guest. Red bumps had appeared all over his penis and testicles. "What's happening?!" he howled.

"I've given you a particularly nasty STD. They call it 'donovanosis'. It starts as deep-red bumps. Gradually, the skin wears away. Eventually, all genital tissue rots. I've accelerated the process, of course."

Ed screamed in agony as the infection did its work.

"You disappoint me, Ed," Abaddon said, taking his jacket from the closet and putting it back on. "More than the rest of them. You had me fooled. For a *split second*, I was considering sparing some of you. How naive I was." He watched as the man's sexual organs disintegrated into nothing. When he was satisfied he'd been tortured enough, he walked past him to vacate the room. "I will leave you to tend to your disfigurement, content in the knowledge that you'll soon burn with the lot of them." He stopped and turned back. "On second thought," He grasped the man by the hair and bashed his skull into the wall, blood and brain matter splattering onto his face. He dropped the body and used his sleeve to wipe his cheek clean. "You don't deserve even one more moment of life."

He left the house, walking peacefully into the night air which was significantly cooler than the day's. He still wasn't at full power and he couldn't risk Lucifer catching up to him before he was. So, he would stay in the confines of this desert town for a little while longer before enacting his plan. That didn't mean, however, that he couldn't have a few laughs while he waited.

"Order up!" a woman yelled from behind the counter. The diner was loud, the voices of dozens of patrons chattering in his ears, the volume like thunder in his head. Abaddon stood near the entrance, watching the people eating happily, discussing this and that as they shoveled in vast quantities of artery-clogging food, blissfully unaware of what would soon befall them. Their gluttony was embarrassing. None showed any consideration for the millions of people that starved right now in their own country, let alone the rest of the world. Worse, still, were the plates of half-eaten food left by consumers whose eyes were bigger than their stomachs. The greed and entitlement of these people knew no bounds. They hoarded resources, growing fat and happy while their fellow man lived in hunger. It was repugnant.

Abaddon gestured with both hands toward the crowd, his mouth curling into a sly smirk. One by one, diner-goers began to hold their stomachs and cover their mouths. Some ran for the bathroom, but most didn't make it. They threw up, vomiting violently onto the floor, into trash cans, and on their plates. A waitress in a yellow, fifties-style uniform attempted to run to the back, but slipped, falling into a puddle of someone's regurgitated dinner. She stood and as she reached for the towel usually used for cleaning the counter, thin, liquid excrement spilled from under her skirt, down her leg, into her shoe, and to the linoleum floor. A look of shocked horror came over her face, but her humiliation lasted only a few seconds as one person after another shared her predicament.

"And their bowels boiled, and would not rest," Abaddon muttered to himself, pleased with the performance of the norovirus.

Chipper conversation had been replaced with screams and retching. None were left clean, most being covered in not only their own filth and sick, but that of their neighbors. Abaddon laughed quietly, exiting the building, the smell repulsive. He put his hands in his pockets and whistled the tune of the commercial for the big box store he'd seen well over a hundred times. It lingered in his brain like lost love and as obnoxious as it was, he couldn't remove it from his thoughts. It didn't matter. Soon, he'd never have to hear it or any of the other insipid melodies created by the human botheration. He looked forward to the only sounds being the waves of the ocean, the wind in the trees, and the rain falling to the ground. "Not long now," he told himself, feeling his strength returning. "Not long at all."

Chapter 21

Will swallowed two acetaminophen tablets along with the last of his soda, setting the empty can on the coffee table, his eyes never leaving the screen. He sat, transfixed, as the fictional town collapsed into the massive crater. Michelle had been right; this *was* a great show.

"Whatever the hell she wants!" he cheered, answering the final question asked by the main character's sister. He got up, went to the entertainment center, and retrieved the DVD from the player. As he placed it back in its case, he felt a white-hot pain shooting from his temple to the back of his head. It was so sharp, it knocked him to his knees. He'd had the same headache for more than a week, but it had been manageable with pain medication. This was different. He'd never felt anything like it before. He winced in pain, putting his hands to his temples as his vision became fuzzy.

Suddenly, he was bombarded with images he couldn't quite make out. There was a bright light, a man in a lab coat coming at him with something metal. Scissors? "Is he okay?" he heard a woman ask. "He's perfect," the man in the coat said. Will was now looking at the face of the woman. He recognized her from pictures and videos his father had shown him. She was his mother. "William," she said. "My angel. I love you so much." She smiled, kissing him on the forehead. She smelled like lavender, her skin soft and warm. She studied his face while he wrapped his tiny fingers around her thumb. "You look just like your fa--" She stopped, her face falling and the light in her eyes fading. She fell back into the hospital bed, the doctor preventing Will from falling as she went limp. The piercing sound of beeps and alarms startled him, causing him to scream and cry as a nurse took him away. He reached his arm out, grasping at the air for his mother, but he could see from the doorway that she wasn't moving, and as the door closed, his delicate, newborn heart was shattered.

Will's vision cleared, the stinging pain in his head replaced by a familiar, dull ache. Tears streamed down his face as the shock of what he'd seen wore off, the realization of what it was gripping him tight. This was a memory; the memory of the day he was born. He was overcome with emotion, covering his mouth with both hands and bawling, never having experienced anything so tragic. It was physically painful, his diaphragm feeling constricted like someone was sitting on it. He wanted to call his father, but he was in an important meeting with suppliers at Pine's, so he sat on the carpet, using his tee shirt to wipe the tears from his face. He knew he couldn't tell Michelle what just happened; she'd think he was either lying or crazy, but he didn't want to be alone. He pulled himself together, gathered up the discs, and headed to the garage. He'd go to her apartment under the guise of bringing her DVDs back and he'd stay there until he felt better, no matter how long it took.

"Will!" Michelle said excitedly, stepping aside to let him in. She closed the door behind him then threw her arms around his neck. "I wasn't expecting to see you today!"

"I just wanted to drop off your DVDs," he said, handing them to her. "It's a really good show. I'll probably start the spin-off tomorrow. You want to come over?"

"Sure!" she bubbled, putting the discs in a cabinet. "Are you okay? Your face looks kind of puffy."

"I'm all right, just a headache."

"Are you sure?"

"Yeah, I'm fine. What have you been up to today?"

"Well, after work, I went to the grocery store, put gas in the car--"

"What was your mom like?" he interrupted. "Sorry, I was just... I was thinking about mine today and how I never got to know her and thought-- never mind. I shouldn't have asked. I don't want to upset you."

"It's fine," she told him, sitting on the couch and waiting for him to sit next to her. When he did, she continued. "Let's see, she was strong-willed and a little impulsive. She married my dad after knowing him for less than three months, which is insane. I mean, who does that, right?"

"I would marry you *tomorrow*," Will confessed. The shock on her face made him immediately regret saying it. "I mean, I'm not proposing. Don't be nervous."

She giggled. "I'm not nervous. I was *going* to say, it sounds crazy to tie yourself to one person forever that soon and I never understood how they could've made that decision. I didn't think love was that strong of an emotion, until I met you."

He looked at her fondly, touching her cheek, tears filling his eyes again as he kissed her. "You know how much I love you, right?" She nodded. "I want you to always know that, okay? No matter what. People die; my mom, your parents, your uncle, but I will *always* be here for you. I will *always* love you."

"You can't make that promise. There are things you don't know. Things that would--"

"I don't care," he professed. "There is nothing you could do, ever, that would make me stop loving you. You have my whole heart."

She kissed him, holding his face in her hands, the tears in his eyes falling to her fingers. She wiped them away and looked inquisitively at the face of this man she just could not get enough of. "Are you sure you're all right? You can tell me anything."

It was nice of her to say, but he knew it wasn't true. If she knew what he was, she would run from him, screaming. "I'm okay," he assured her. She nodded and kissed him again, leaning her body into his. She sat up, preparing to straddle him. Just then, he got another stabbing pain in his left temple. It burned through his skull like fire, a cloud of images once again flooding his mind.

He gently pushed her away and put his hand to his head. "I have a headache," he said.

"Are you kidding?"

"No," he declared, getting up and walking quickly to the door. "I need to go take some pain medicine."

"I have some here," she offered.

"That's okay, I need to go home, anyway. Dinner with my dad. I'll see you tomorrow? Around seven?"

"Sure," she agreed.

He left the apartment, not one hundred percent sure if he'd closed the door all the way. He stumbled down the stairs and out the lobby doors to the parking lot. He hadn't made it to his car when the memories overtook him. He dropped to the sidewalk, clutching his head in anguish, flashes of memory after memory filling his brain, the real world disappearing from view. He trembled, his mind unable to process this much information so quickly. Blood trickled from his nose as he toppled over, his head hitting the pavement with a ghastly thud. He laid there, shaking, as the sun set on the horizon. Michelle, oblivious, searched her closet for an outfit to wear to her date tomorrow, excited to spend more time with her beloved.

Chapter 22

Death rose like steam from the streets as Lucifer walked through the Old City. Blister-covered bodies lay everywhere, some still clutching phones or grocery bags. "Leprosy," he uttered, covering his nose, the stench of decay making him gag. He hadn't seen a plague like this in thirty-five hundred years. Disease that struck down this many people this swiftly could only be Abaddon's doing. He searched high and low but turned up nothing. He knew what he was planning. "A weapon to wipe out all of humanity." He leaped into the sky, flying out of Israel and back to Gabriel's apartment. He was going to need her help.

"Ada!" fifteen-year-old Gabriel screamed from the road, watching in horror as the building burned. Security guards threw her in the back of a town car and sped off as she sobbed, the cries of her friends still ringing in her ears.

"That must have been unbearable," a guard said, a menacing smile creeping across his face.

"What?" she asked.

"Tell me, did you know it was them, or did you go years thinking it was an electrical malfunction as the investigation implied?"

"This is a dream," she realized, her current visage replacing her teenage self.

"Yes, and you'll be waking soon, undoubtedly full of self-righteous indignation and contempt, but, I want to be clear, you can not defeat me and you shouldn't want to."

"Uh-huh," she dismissed.

"Think about it, Gabriel. These people are little more than vessels of malfeasance, destroying without a thought what our Father so graciously gave them. They kill each other and this planet with no remorse. I've spent weeks trying to find *anyone* worth redemption. *One person* worthy of sparing. I could find no one. They are flawed, resentful, and angry. They hate for sport. They do not deserve life."

"Yeah, people are generally trash cans."

"So, you agree?"

"No one's *perfect*," she told him. "I mean, *shit*, I've known *my whole life* the secrets of the universe; God and Heaven, Purgatory, all of human history, and I'm *severely fucked up*. Imagine having none of that knowledge, just guessing and hoping, clawing around in the dark for something that felt like right. People are wild animals with souls pulling them in a direction they don't understand. They're just trying their best."

"They are failing."

"They are orphans of the Throne, just waiting to get back home."

"As are you?" he asked. "Wouldn't you like to go back to where you belong?"

"You think I'd be welcome if I stood by and let you blow the planet to shit?"

"God would forgive you. He always does."

"You know He loves them, right? Like, *a lot*."

"He will start over when He wakes," he sighed. "This time, giving them proper instructions."

"Last time He told them what to do, it didn't work out so well."

"Their stupidity is egregious. How difficult is it to love one another? How confusing is kindness?"

"I'm picking up what you're putting down, but I still can't let you kill them."

"You've been among them too long," he griped. "You're weak. Your subconscious is riddled with childhood traumas. Your mind is tormented by guilt over things you can not change and you, like Lucifer, are obedient to a Father that puts you second, preferring these primates to His first-born."

"Can we wrap this up? I'm losing interest."

"You will not stop me."

"You think?"

"Your human body lessens your abilities, I'm sure. In your current state, you have no chance against me."

"In my current state, bitch, I'm *Irish*. I will cut you like soap."

Gabriel woke to find Lucifer standing over her bed, impatience covering his face. "Let me guess," he said. "Abaddon infiltrating your dreams?"

"Yeah, he tried to give me the whole 'they deserve it' speech," she sneered, getting up and heading to the kitchen. She put two frozen waffles in the toaster and opened a can of soda.

"Somehow, your eating habits never fail to disturb me," he snorted, peeling himself a banana.

"Dude, it is four in the morning. I need caffeine."

"Most people drink coffee."

"Most people hate themselves." She dumped an unnecessary amount of syrup on her now plated breakfast and began to eat.

"That's disgusting."

"It's delicious."

"Why do you eat so much sugar, sister? You must know it's unhealthy."

"Dopamine."

"Yes, well, do hurry. Abaddon's already released a plague on Jerusalem and I think you can guess where his next stop is."

"I know. I've been keeping an eye. I gave him a chance to change his mind, but--"

"You what?!"

"He hadn't hurt anyone until now. Waited til I was asleep. Pretty smart. Or maybe just lucky."

"Either way, this fight could get rather messy. Are you sure you're up for it?"

She finished her waffles and downed the rest of her beverage before responding, "Oh, if this motherfucker wants to *go*, we'll *go*."

Chapter 23

Valerie paced the living room floor, her siblings having woken her when they left, off to who knows where to do who knows what. She was staying in Wyatt's old room, unnerved by the fact that she was sharing a bedroom wall with the Devil. Gabriel had assured her that he was behaving himself since coming back, and he had given her a nice honeymoon, showing a more thoughtful side of himself that she didn't know existed before. Maybe he wasn't *so* bad. *Maybe.*

The sun wouldn't be up for half an hour and she wasn't due back at work until next week. "Fuck this," she muttered, picking up her bong from the bar and grabbing a lighter. She would smoke herself sleepy and go back to bed, saving the stress of her probable divorce for a later time. As she put her mouth to the glass, there was a soft knock at the door. "Who's there?" she called, expecting to have to shoo away one of her sister's many companions.

"It's Malik!" said the voice from the other side. She put her things down and ran to let him in.

"Baby!" she cheered. "How'd you know where I was?"

"When you weren't home, I figured you came here. I hoped, anyway."

She embraced him, kissing him for several seconds before he pulled away.

"Stop, stop," he told her, holding her at arm's length. "We've got to talk about this. Now, I've calmed down, but you've got to explain this to me."

"Okay," she agreed, closing the door behind him and following him to the sofa. "Ask me anything."

"Demons. How big of a problem are they? Are they everywhere? Are we gonna get jumped again?"

"No, Lucifer put them all back in Hell. There won't be another one on Earth for at least two hundred and forty years."

"And Lucifer's *Lucifer*, Lucifer?"

"I mean, yeah."

"And he's what, their king?"

"Shit, no. He's more like a prison guard."

"But he's the Devil, like, the fucking Devil."

"He's harmless to you."

"*Harmless*? We were *attacked by a demon* and you're telling me *Satan* is *harmless*?"

"Oh, he's scary as shit, but he won't hurt you, I swear. I mean, I can't say he *never* kills people, but--"

"What the fuck, Val?!"

"Racists, homophobes, misogynists, all kinds of bigots; that's who needs to be worried about pissing him off. I'm not saying it's cool, but I can understand where he's coming from. He hasn't killed anybody in years, though, so--"

"You're defending *Lucifer* to me now?"

"I'm as surprised as you are, but he *is* my brother."

"Your *what*?"

"I told you I'm an angel. Were you not listening?"

"It must not have registered while I was bandaging up the bite wounds I got fending off a fucking *demon*."

"You remember the blond dude at the wedding? The one that left before the reception? That was him."

"Satan was at our wedding?"

"Yeah, and see? Everything was fine."

"This is a lot for me, baby," he sighed.

"I understand, but you're focusing on the negative shit. Hell's real, but so is Heaven. I'm a fucking angel. I've got superpowers and shit. You have got *nothing* to worry about."

"What does that mean, though? Is 'Valerie' just an act for you?"

"No, 'Valerie' is who I am. I was born and I grew up like everybody else. My experiences and genetics formed my personality. Uriel is me *inside*. It's like, normal people have souls that act as their conscience. Uriel is that for me. The instinct to do the right thing, the moral compass, that sort of thing. And, when my body dies, Uriel will go back to Heaven, remembering everything about this life, just like a human soul would."

"I'm gonna have to think on this," he told her. "The Lucifer thing freaks me out, I'm not gonna lie, but that's just a small part of it. I'm sayin', I'm *nothing* compared to you. I don't have special abilities, I don't have thousands of years of stories to tell. I'm just a man. How could I ever be enough for you?"

"Baby," she chortled, touching his cheek. "I'm an angel, but I'm human, too. I love you more than I've ever loved anyone. You might be a regular-ass man, but you're fine as hell, you lay down that d like none other *and* you can cook. I could comb the universe and never find anything better than that."

He laughed. "I just don't want to disappoint you."

"You could never disappoint me," she said, kissing him gently.

"Wait, wait, wait. So, your sister is Gabriel from the *Bible*?"

"I guess we're not done talking."

Chapter 24

Wyatt awoke much groggier than usual. He felt heavy, his limbs like stone. He turned off his alarm and slowly crept down the stairs, eager to get some coffee in his system. When he got to the kitchen, he found Will already awake and making breakfast.

"Hey, Dad," he said, flipping something in a pan on the stove. "I think I've got this pancake thing down. I put a touch of vanilla in the batter. You sleep okay? You look terrible."

"I just need some coffee," Wyatt slurred, pouring himself a cup, grateful for his son's skills in the kitchen. "And send two of those pancakes my way."

"No problem," Will said, placing them on a plate and setting it on the table. "There's also bacon in the oven. It'll be a couple of minutes."

"Thanks, buddy." He chugged his first cup and poured another, ignoring the heat that scorched the roof of his mouth. He took the syrup from the pantry and as he sat to eat, his phone rang.

"Hello?" he answered.

"Is this Wyatt?" the voice on the other end asked.

"Yes."

"Hello, Wyatt. This is Bob Wilkins. You may not remember me. I'm your father's lawyer. We met twenty years ago or so when you--"

"I remember," Wyatt said, recalling the incident in college when he'd destroyed his dorm room in what he thought had been a psychotic episode. A window, bed frame, and desk had been broken. Bob convinced the university to settle, ensuring that Wyatt would be able to finish school there.

"Of course," The lawyer cleared his throat before continuing. "I'm sorry to be the one to tell you this, but, last night, your father passed away."

"What?" Wyatt stood and walked to the living room, not wanting Will to hear. "What happened?"

"The doctor called it 'ventricular fibrillation', but that's just a fancy way of saying 'heart attack'. I'm sorry, son."

"Do you know if," Wyatt choked, unable to hide the quiver in his voice. "Was it painful?"

"It was very quick. He most likely felt a sharp jolt for a couple of seconds before losing consciousness. A neighbor found him and called an ambulance right away, but--"

"Okay."

"Everything's been taken care of. After the first heart attack a few years ago, he put a plan together. All I have to do is execute it. He wanted it over with as fast as possible, so your grief wouldn't be dragged out."

"He was nothing if not efficient."

"The funeral's today at one. Most of his belongings will be boxed up and donated next week, but there are a few sentimental things he wanted you to have, along with the rest of the estate."

"Sentimental? We are talking about *my* father?"

Bob chuckled. "I'll leave them for you in his-- *your* apartment. I'll text you the funeral details."

"All right, thank you, Bob."

"Of course, son. I know you've moved out of state. Will I see you this afternoon?"

"Yeah, it's only a two and a half hour flight. I'll be there."

"Okay, see you then."

Wyatt ended the call and looked back into the kitchen where Will sat, speedily eating what must have been his sixth pancake. He didn't know how to tell him. He didn't *want* to tell him. News like this could trigger him, potentially causing him to lose control. He couldn't risk it. He'd go to the funeral alone and tell Will what happened when he got back.

"Dad?" Will said, noticing the tears building in Wyatt's eyes. He got up from the table and went to his father. "Dad, are you okay?"

Wyatt pulled his son in for a hug, letting one tear fall to his cheek and wiping it away, suppressing the emotion he was feeling. "I'm fine," he said, pulling away. "I have to go to the city. I'll try to make it back by tonight. Stay here, okay? Promise me you'll stay here."

"Michelle's coming over later to watch TV, but if we get hungry--"

"I'll leave pizza money. Just don't leave the house. I mean it. If something happened to you, I don't know how I'd--"

"Okay," Will promised. "Okay, I'll stay here while you're gone. Are you sure you're all right? You do not look 'fine'."

"We'll talk about it when I get home. I'll be okay, I swear. As long as you stay safe."

"I'll do my best."

Wyatt stood over his father's fresh grave, the loneliness of being the last mourner to leave like rocks in his gut. He had been fine throughout the service, cold and stoic, showing no emotion whatsoever. Now, though, the sinking in his stomach was too much. He could no longer stifle the tears that fell hot on his cheeks in the afternoon sun that shone too bright to be tolerated by a man missing his father.

"I should have called more," he bleated. "I should have made more of an effort." He stared at the headstone, his tears blurring his vision so much that he could no longer make out the inscription. "There were things I couldn't tell you, that I really wanted to. What I am, what I can do. That what I was seeing weren't hallucinations. That I talked to Mom. And you were right, she was really beautiful. I didn't tell you that you have a grandson or that he's a genius, taking classes for three degrees at the same time. Now, he'll never get to know his grandfather. I took that from him because I didn't want to scare you. I finally felt like I was more than a burden to you and I didn't want that to end, so, I'm sorry. I'm sorry I didn't trust you with who I am." He walked around the mound of earth, placed a hand on the cool, smooth granite of the headstone, and knelt next to it as if telling it a secret. "I wish you were here."

Wyatt sat on the sofa in his father's living room, the silence of the apartment suffocating. He loosened his tie and rolled his sleeves up before examining the contents of the boxes Bob had left on the coffee table for him. Pictures of his mother, his parents' wedding album, and his father's music collection were what had meant the most to the old man and Wyatt was thankful to have them now. He put a CD in the stereo and quietly played "Here There and Everywhere" as he flipped through the photo album, taking note of how happy his father looked. He'd never in his life seen his dad smile like that. It was jarring and comforting at the same time. "At least you're together now," he muttered. He set the book aside and found another small, leather album at the bottom of the box. He was astonished upon opening it to see pictures of himself as a child; baby pictures, school pictures, and a few from his wedding to Annie. He didn't know his father had kept any of them. Tears again began to build. He stood and paced the hardwood floor, the sound of his steps echoing as he thought about the first time he'd left Will home alone. He'd spent so much time worrying if his son would be all right that he hadn't really enjoyed the visit. John talked mostly about work and they discussed the possibility of franchising Pine's, which Wyatt had no intention of doing, though the idea was intriguing. They'd joked about Indiana weather and the use of the word 'ope'. John didn't have one drink that day and Wyatt had been glad to see his father taking better care of himself. Not better enough, though, apparently.

A knock on the door broke Wyatt from his memory and he answered it, forgetting to turn the stereo off.

"Do you want to be alone?" Allydia asked. He shook his head and let her in. She removed her cloak, a necessity she wore, even in the June heat, as it was still day. He closed the door and went back to turn off the music. "Leave it," she requested. "I love this song." He did and returned to his seat on the couch. "I heard about your father."

"How?"

"I have people."

"Right."

"I'm very sorry."

"Thank you."

"Are you all right?"

"I'm okay, just," he sighed, the heaviness of the day making him feel weak. "I don't know how to deal with this. How did you?"

"How did I what?" she asked, sitting next to him.

"Deal with losing your parents."

"You mean my mother? She died when I was two, so I don't remember what that was like. I'm sorry I can't give you any advice on the matter."

"What about your father?"

"Cain? He's cursed to eternally wander the Earth, never able to stay in one place for more than--"

"Your dad's *Cain*? Like, Cain and Abel, Cain?"

"I thought you knew."

"How would I have known?"

"If your siblings didn't tell you, I would have thought my surname made it clear."

"I honestly thought you'd made that up."

"What?"

"Because it sounds…never mind."

"I did drop the 'ibnat'. Being called 'daughter' seemed disingenuous, after."

"Cain. Well, that is just…something."

"Can I get you anything? Water? Food?"

"No, I'm fine, thank you, though. It's nice of you to come by."

"I have ulterior motives," she admitted.

"Don't you always?"

"I know this isn't the appropriate time, but, I'd like to speak to you about our," She thought for a moment. "Whatever we are."

"You want to have the 'where is this going' talk *now*?"

"Not especially, but I feel I must say this before I get…frisky."

He chuckled. "Go ahead."

She moved to sit on the table in front of him to better look into his face as she spoke. "I don't know what this feeling is. I was married in my previous life, before I was what I am. I loved my husband and I was bereaved when he died. I was grief-stricken when my children were taken from me. I lamented for months. But, I've never been as devastated as I was when you left. I spent more than three years confined to my private room, unable to hunt or feed. Some days I couldn't drink at all. I made myself sick missing you. What I feel for you is stronger than I know how to handle. According to your sister, you feel as though no one has ever put you and your needs first, but *I do*. I will *always* put you ahead of *anyone*, including myself. That's why I want to give you the choice. I know what it's like for men to be near me. I don't want you to feel tricked into being with me. If we're together, it has to be because you wish it so and if you want me to go, I'll go. You'll never have to see me again if that's what you prefer. But, if you want me, I will never leave your side."

He stared at her, awestruck and mute, his mind swirling with the emotions of the day. His silence lasted too long, a clear indication to Allydia that she should leave with what remained of her dignity. "I understand," she told him, getting up and walking toward the door. She opened it slightly, but it slammed in front of her.

She turned to find Wyatt standing over her, his eyes like fire burning through her. He brushed the hair away from her eyes, watching them as they watched him, sparkling in the dimly lit room and beginning to dilate. Unabashed happiness filled her as the hushed command left his lips, "Don't go."

Chapter 25

Will swallowed the acetaminophen, his third dose of the day. His headache was getting worse and with it, flashes of memories he had no business remembering. He pushed them away and ordered pizza in preparation for his date with Michelle. He tied the bag of trash that filled the kitchen garbage can and took it outside where he stopped to admire the early evening sky, painted in varying shades of red and orange. He'd just turned to go back inside when he heard it...the low, quiet growl of a wolf.

Two gray wolves stepped out of the woods, then six more. They crept toward him, snarling and baring their teeth. He moved to run back into the house but was blocked by another wolf, this one larger than the others with a darker coat. It howled in his face, a signal to the rest of the pack, before leaping at him, knocking him to the ground. It stood upon his chest, howling once more. They all came at him at once, biting his back and legs as he went fetal, instinctively protecting his neck, chest, and stomach. The pain was blinding. He knew if he didn't do something soon, he'd die, so he managed to get up on his knees and begin to fight back.

He grasped the mouth of one of the beasts and pried its jaws apart, snapping the bone. It yelped, backing off a bit, but not surrendering. He threw another one off of him, sending it flying all the way to the roof of the barn. He stood, waiting, hoping he had scared them enough that they'd now run away. They didn't. Following the big one's lead, they came for him again, clamping down on his arms and legs, rendering him immobile. He glanced around wildly, the amount of blood that covered the animals and himself, all of it his, was alarming. He'd lost too much and was beginning to feel dizzy. Terror set in as the pack's leader approached him, its eyes fixed on his now exposed throat. Adrenaline rushed through his veins, his heart pounding in his ears like a drum. His mind went blank. No plan could be made to get himself out of this. They had him. He was sure he was going to die.

As the wolf lunged, Will could feel something hot inside him, rising like steam from his solar plexus to just under his skin. It burned like acid as it spewed from him out of every pore, a wave of white lightning, bursting out in all directions, killing all eight of the wolves instantaneously. Their bodies dropped, singed and smoking.

Will fell to his knees, hurt and trembling, horrified by what he'd done. "You had no choice," he told himself, catching his breath. "They would've killed you. You *had* to."

He got to his feet, hunger replacing fear, and hurried inside where he took several slices of bread from the package and gorged himself, devouring one after another until there was none left in the bag. Blood dripped from his arms to the floor, leaving small puddles everywhere he went. Suddenly, his headache went from bad to intolerable, shooting through the nerves like a bullet on fire. He dropped to the floor, more memories flooding his mind. He remembered Gabriel telling his father that she should kill him and seeing the fear in her eyes as she looked down at him through the car window. He remembered his mother's voice when she'd spoken to him while he was in the womb, her guilt about hiding him from his father, and explaining her reasons for doing it. He remembered being born. Tears fell like water from a faucet from his bloodshot eyes, the memories more painful than his wounds. He went to take his phone from his pocket, desperate to call his dad, but it wasn't there. It must have fallen out during the fight. He slapped himself in the face, trying to free himself of the visions that ran rampant in his brain, but he couldn't shake them. They kept coming, clouding his judgement and whittling at his sanity. He was so lost in his head that he didn't hear the front door open or the knocking that had come before.

"Will?" Michelle called. "Will!" She crouched next to him on the tile floor, taking his face in her hands. "What happened? Will, what happened? Talk to me."

"They attacked me," he told her, his shaky voice barely above a whisper.

"Who did?"

"Wolves."

"What? Okay," she said, calming herself and examining the gashes, bite marks, and places where entire chunks of flesh had been torn out. "Okay, come on. We have to get you to a hospital. Can you stand?"

"I'm not going anywhere."

"Will," she pleaded.

"I promised my dad I'd stay here until he got back. It shouldn't be long."

"Will, we can call your dad from the car. Please!"

"You should go."

"Are you crazy?! I'm not leaving you like this. You could die!"

"There's only one thing that kills something like me."

She backed off, noticing a change in his tone. "Will, you're scaring me."

"I don't want to," he said, tears again forming in his eyes. "I don't want to hurt anyone. I don't want to hurt *you*, Michelle. You're--" He paused. "You know what you are to me. I'm not okay. So, go, please. Please, just go."

She nodded, wiping tears from her cheeks and kissing him gently before getting up and leaving the house, calling Gabriel from the porch. No answer. As she hurried to her car, she passed the pizza delivery man on the long sidewalk. "Run," she warned him, not breaking her stride. He gave her a puzzled look and continued to the front door as she drove off. He knocked a few times before growing impatient and letting himself in.

"Hello?" the twenty-something-year-old man called. "Pizza! Anyone here?"

Will staggered to the living room. "You have to go," he commanded. "Leave the pizza."

"Dude! Are you okay?! You need an ambulance?" He took his phone from his pocket and started to call nine-one-one.

"No ambulance," Will said.

"You need a hospital, bro," the man insisted, putting the phone to his ear.

"I said 'no'," Will grunted, shoving him to the ground, the pizza box falling open, spilling its contents onto the carpet. *"I can't leave."*

"What the fuck?! Man, you need help. You're lucky you're already fucked up because if you weren't hurt, I'd kick your scrawny ass myself. Now, I'm calling an ambulance, like it or not."

"I can't let you do that," Will insisted, kicking the man in the face, sending blood and teeth flying. "They'd take me to the hospital, which means I wouldn't be here when my dad gets home and I promised him *I'd stay here."* He knocked the man unconscious with one blow to the top of the head. Worried he'd gone too far, he checked that he was still breathing. When he could feel the warm air coming from the man's gaping mouth, he relaxed, sitting next to him on the floor. He moved the pizza box to the coffee table, out of the way of the food that lay in a mangled pile on the carpet, and started eating directly from the floor, the pangs of hunger now completely overwhelming.

Chapter 26

"Okay, I'm chartering a jet for the trip back. That was *unpleasant*," Gabriel griped after Lucifer set her on her feet.

"Agreed," he said. "Flying with a passenger isn't my cup of tea, either, especially when they're squirming."

"Dude, it was *really* high."

"Yes, well, it cut our travel time by half, and as you can see, time is of the essence."

The fly-covered bodies that lined the streets had taken on a foul stench so putrid, even stray animals stayed away.

"I'm gonna throw up," Gabriel complained, covering her mouth. "No, no, I'm good. Let's just find this asshole so we can get home. I think I left my phone on the counter. *Or* I dropped it somewhere over Ireland."

"You're worried about social media *now*?"

"There could be an emergency."

"A bigger emergency than *this*?" he gestured to the decomposing Israelis that littered the pavement like confetti after a parade.

"Apples and oranges."

"What on Earth could be more pressing than preventing humanity's complete annihilation by way of nuclear missile?"

"Probably nothing, but--" Just then, a far-off buzzing filled the air. "The fuck is that?"

"He knows we're here," Lucifer surmised. The sound grew louder, the high-pitched screech roaring above them. They could see now that the noise came from what must have been millions of locusts, the wall of them so dense, it blotted out the sun. The sound was deafening as they descended, swarming, covering the siblings in suits of living hum.

"Can you do something about this, please?!" Gabriel yelled. Lucifer forced the insects off of them, sending them high into the air. He drew them to each other, the buzzing of their wings replaced by the crunch of their bodies as they were compelled together. Lucifer enforced his will on them, driving them to commit suicide by flight until no sound remained. The ball of macerated bug parts fell to the ground in front of them with a sickening, wet thud. "That's fucking gross," Gabriel observed. "But I appreciate you."

They'd started walking, heading to the not-so-secret site of Israel's nuclear weapons stash when they heard a rustling behind them followed by a deep moan. They turned to see the dead rising, their vacant, unsettling stares more unnerving than the haphazard way with which they shuffled toward them.

"Are you serious right now?" Gabriel whined. "I forgot he can make zombies. Pain in my ass."

"Would you mind, sister?" Lucifer asked, motioning toward the dozens of ghouls approaching them from all sides. "I'd like to save my strength for the main event."

"Yeah, I'm just waiting for them to get a good distance from the buildings." She crossed her arms as they drew nearer.

"We have little time to waste," he scolded.

"I am not about to destroy a city block over a few creepers."

"I see over a hundred, which I would venture to say counts as a horde. And, might I remind you, that while they may not be able to kill you permanently, if they liberate a limb from your body, it will not grow back."

"Fine," she sighed, rolling her eyes. She waved her hands up to her shoulders, engulfing the mob in flames. Some fell instantly while others continued, mindlessly staggering onward until they, too, dropped a few feet away from where the two stood.

"Well done," Lucifer praised. "And you managed to avoid any structures. Now, on to Dimona."

The site appeared desolate. It was Chernobyl in its silence. They entered the facility, the cold sterility of the military installation cutting through them like shards of glass. The lights were all on and computers remained opened on the oversized, oval table that sat in front of a wall of screens. To their right was a control panel, its lights flashing and a timer counting down the seconds until the launch. 29, 28, 27. To their left, a man sat, listless on the floor, propped against a wall of clocks. He had a rash, a nosebleed, and had very clearly recently vomited on himself. 26, 25, 24.

"What disease is *that*?" Lucifer cringed.

"Dengue fever," Gabriel told him, bending down to heal the dying man, whose temperature had run up to a hundred and ten degrees.

23, 22, 21, 20.

"Is now the best time for that?" Lucifer prodded.

"Hey, I may be a garbage human, but I'm not heartless."

19, 18, 17

"I never implied tha--"

The man jumped up, terror on his face and gratitude in his eyes. He ran off, being of no help in their current predicament. 16, 15, 14.

"Wonderful," Lucifer exasperated, the counter ticking down. 13, 12, 11, 10, 9. "How do we stop it?"

"I got it," Gabriel assured, flipping the correct switches and ending the sequence. "You didn't think I knew how to shut down a nuclear launch?"

"Honestly, sister, I didn't believe it would be that easy."

"Well, we're not done yet, are we?"

"No, we're not. Remember, when we find Abaddon--"

"Yeah, yeah. Hold him in his body so you can beat his ass. Seems like a time suck, but whatever you want."

"Now to find the miscreant."

"I can hear him," Gabriel said, pointing to her temple. "Underground bunker. Guess he didn't want to ruin his man-suit killing off the rest of the planet. Honestly, he thinks nothing through. Like, how did he *not know* that blowing up the planet with fucking nuclear hell-fire would devastate *everything*? Plants, animals. This dumb motherfucker thought he'd just get rid of people and the rest of nature would be *fine*.

He'd have all the food and clean water he could handle, living in a new Garden of fucking Eden, all alone until God woke up. Stupid as *shit*."

"Yes, he's always been emotional, reason never playing much of a role in his decision making."

They got in the elevator and headed down to the underground bomb shelter where they found Abaddon, genuinely surprised that they'd found him.

"You're too late," he told them. "Any second, the bombs will fall. I have one pointed at every major city on Earth. Soon, this world will be free of the human scourge and you wi--"

"Yeah, I shut that shit *right* the fuck down," Gabriel declared. "No explosions today. Sorry, bro."

"You did *what*?!"

"A few switches here, a couple button pushes there. It wasn't hard."

"I will tear your foul tongue from your mouth and use it to strangle the life from you, once and for all."

"Give it a shot," she goaded. He rushed toward her, but she held her arm out, throwing him back with the power of her mind. "You know, I understand the child molester thing. That piece of shit got what he deserved. But the diner people? That was just rude." She flicked a finger in his direction causing a gash to appear on his left cheek. He winced, staring angrily at her while she smiled. "I told you," she giggled. "*Like soap*."

"Gabriel," Lucifer scolded. "Remember what we talked about."

"Lucifer, from God's favorite son to His biggest disappointment," Abaddon poked. "Imagine how angry He'll be."

"He'll get over it," Gabriel interjected.

"Now, Gabriel, you know how He can get."

"Bitch, I don't know what you're talking for. You must have forgotten how *I* can get." She started to raise her hand, but Lucifer held it down.

"This fight is mine, sister."

"Are you sure? I can just--"

"Yes, but I've waited a long time for this."

"All right," she grumbled, again lifting her hand and making a fist.

"What are you doing?" Abaddon accused.

"Call it a cage match," she smirked.

He needed to get back to the control room and restart the launch sequence. He would then handle these two. He tried to teleport but realized he could not. She had bound him, rendering him trapped, unable to leave this body or to transmit it to another location. Now a fair fight, Lucifer pounced, landing a hard right hook into his brother's eye. He went down, touching his face and laughing.

"You want to fight this way?" he jeered. "Like these creatures our Father takes so much pride in? Like *animals*?"

"I find it cathartic," Lucifer commented. "The Gates are closed. There's no redemption for you to be had. This ends now."

"So be it," Abaddon growled, getting to his feet. "But, how can you be sure that it will be *my* end and not the two of yours?"

Gabriel snickered.

"*You* against God's most powerful angel and a firestarter?" Lucifer scoffed. "You wouldn't stand less of a chance if you were human." He punched him again, breaking his nose, and again, cracking his cheekbone, and again, breaking his jaw. Abaddon fought back, throwing punishing blows to Lucifer's stomach and face. They went back and forth, exchanging jabs, both of them bloody and broken.

"Are you done yet?" Gabriel whined. "My arm's getting tired."

They continued to brawl, pushing each other into walls, smashing screens, and putting holes in the concrete. Lucifer, growing tired, lifted Abaddon over his head and slammed him through a table, sending bits of metal flying in all directions and shattering most of his enemy's vertebra. He was unconscious, his ability to heal slowed by the amount of punishment Lucifer had inflicted.

Lucifer left him, looked to his sister, and walked from the room, telling her breathlessly as he passed, "Go ahead." She turned to follow him and flicked her wrist behind her, igniting the angel in flames so hot, he was completely incinerated within seconds, his body and the true form within it gone before the sprinklers turned on.

"That wasn't so difficult," Lucifer remarked, peering out the window of the small jet as it took off.

"I told you we wouldn't need the others," Gabriel reminded.

"Speaking of the others, why have you been so secretive about our dear brother's whereabouts? Uriel doesn't even know his location and the two of you are thick as thieves. I admit, though I've been preoccupied, I have been curious."

"I can't tell you."

"Come, now. I just helped you save the world...*again*. You can trust me. I won't tell a soul."

"No."

"Fine, then answer something else for me, because I don't quite understand. Wyatt, emotional powder keg though he may be, is a grown man. Why are you so protective of him? *He* was the one of us created for protecting others. Why do you baby him so?"

"I owe him."

"For what?"

"It's my fault," she confessed. "Everything wrong with him, psychologically, is because of me. You feel guilty about closing the Gate and staying here. You feel like you failed God. Well, I failed Wyatt. I failed him *hard*."

"You can't blame yourself for his afflictions. You didn't know where he was for *decades*."

"I did. I did know, once. When I was fifteen, I saw him at a party. I could feel him. I *knew* it was him, but I didn't say anything. I don't even think he saw me. I just let him walk by. I didn't tell him who he was because I was *too high to care*. He spent twenty years thinking he was insane, being locked up in institutions and drugged, his friends abandoning him. His wife left him, his dad treated him like trash. You don't know *half* of the fucked up shit he's been through and all of it was because I let my personal bullshit matter more than the mission. I know that he's not the Barachiel you remember and I know you miss him, but he's in there. Under all that pain and anger and depression, the brother you know is *in there*. You know as well as I do that he's the best of us, and I fucked him up, so, yeah, I baby him a little. I worry about him. I let him get away with things I know I shouldn't. I let him make mistakes because I don't want to be the one to hurt him again, but, *shit*. What would *you* do, if you were me?"

"Me?" Lucifer considered. "I'd probably drown my sorrows in gluttonous amounts of alcohol and women, followed by years of regret and self-loathing."

"Bro, you just described my twenties."

Chapter 27

Will tossed the last wolf's body onto the pile, covered the heap in lighter fluid he'd gotten from under the grill, backed away, and chucked a ball of lightning at it. The mound of corpses erupted in a plume of smoke and flame, the fire growing hotter the more it consumed. He went back inside for a snack, his hunger raging once more. He opened a new package of bread and made a sandwich, then another. He was so hungry that eventually, he stopped assembling and ate the ingredients separately, shoving lunch meat, cheese, and bread in his mouth as fast as his hands would allow. More memories flooded his brain, these not even his own. They were his mother's memories and they were brutal. He knew what she had been thinking and feeling when he was developing inside of her. He could see his father through her eyes, throwing furniture and breaking mirrors, screaming nonsense. She was afraid of him.

Will made his way up the stairs, deciding he should get cleaned up before his dad got home, but as he reached the landing, a wave of pain hit him so hard, he collapsed. Blood poured from his nose as more memories cascaded in. They seared his brain like a hot poker, causing him to convulse. Visions of his childhood, his mother's voice, and the fear in his aunt's eyes flashed like cameras. He cried out, his hands gripping the sides of his head. He hyperventilated as he seized, his nervous system overloaded with information. He opened his mouth to scream again, but just as the sound was about to escape his throat, everything went dark. He was limp, his breathing shallow, his heart barely beating.

Wyatt drove up to the house, stopping before reaching the driveway. He and Allydia watched as the pizza delivery man ran out the front door and got into his car, speeding off, nearly taking out the mailbox as he went. The two got out of the car, immediately getting soaked by the rain that fell hard from the night sky. Wyatt could smell fire and went around the house to find a smoldering pile of ash in the backyard. He couldn't tell what had been destroyed there, but whatever it was, it had been big.

Allydia entered the house first, a feeling of unease washing over her. "Wyatt," she all but whispered as he came in behind her, her eyes dilating and hunger pulling her toward the stairs. "Wyatt, I smell blood."

He moved past her and darted up the stairs to find his son, bleeding and unresponsive. "Will," he croaked. "Will!" He shook him, but nothing. He listened for a heartbeat. It was there, but it was slow. There was no time to get him to the hospital. He'd have to heal him himself. He placed his hands on the boy, one on his head and one on his heart, and concentrated.

"What are you doing?" Allydia asked.

"I'm trying to heal him."

"Do you know how to do that?"

"Not a clue," he admitted. "But I've seen Gabriel do it. I've seen Barachiel do it. I just have to focus." He thought about the memory Valerie had shown him years before, where he'd healed the boy in the alley. He thought about how that had felt and tried to recreate it. "Come on," he cried. "Come on!" Finally, white light glowed from his hands. Will's skin, too, began to illuminate, the marks on his arms shrinking and disappearing. Will sprung up, clutching his chest and coughing, the sudden rush of air in his lungs painful.

Wyatt leaned against the wall, exhausted and weak, the healing taking all of his strength.

"Dad?" Will panted, looking down at his arms. "Did you fix me? I didn't know you could do that."

"Neither did I," Wyatt wheezed, finding it difficult to catch his breath, as well. "What the hell happened?" He sat on the stairs, leaning against the railing. He glanced down to the living room where he saw Allydia, hovering near the front door, looking afraid.

"I'm a monster is what happened," Will answered, tears welling in his eyes. "I'm not okay, Dad. You should've let Gabriel kill me when she had the chance."

"How do you know about that? Did she talk to you? She had no right--"

"I remember it," Will bellowed, jumping up and heading down the stairs, ignoring the vampire's cautious stare. "I remember everything. I remember my mom talking to me before I was born. I remember how she felt when you'd go off the rails, how afraid she was. I remember how, despite that, she almost didn't have me so she could stay with you. She made an appointment and everything, but I grew too fast."

Wyatt teetered down the stairs to join the others, lightheaded, his balance unsteady. "I'm sure that's not true," he challenged. "I knew your mother. She wouldn't--"

"She would have," Will asserted. "She would have for *you*. And I wish she had because knowing I killed her is--"

"You *didn't* kill her."

"I did. I did, Dad. I *remember* it. *I tore that woman apart.* She didn't give birth to me, I *fled* her. I could hear her heart above me getting weaker. I could feel her pulse getting fainter. If I didn't get out, I would have been dead, so I left. And after everything I put her through, she asked the doctor if *I* was okay. She was worried about *me*. She loved me, and I watched her die. I'm a monster that never should have been born."

"You're not a monster," Wyatt choked. "You're a good kid. You're smart and caring and--"

"I'm not a kid anymore, Dad, and I'm *not* good. You have no idea what I've done." He opened the door to the garage and slammed it behind him. Wyatt tried to follow, the muffled sound of Will's car starting giving him a sense of urgency, but Allydia stood in his way.

"Move," he demanded.

"What are you doing?"

"I'm going after him, what do you think?"

"You're spent. You're in no condition. You should call your sister."

"Get out of my way, Allydia."

"You can't move me unless I allow it. I'm stronger than you, especially in your current condition, so unless you're planning on electrocuting me--"

"He's my son."

"He's dangerous. He's killed someone. He wears the stench of death like cologne."

"Did you see him?! He was obviously attacked."

"Wyatt,"

"And how many people have you killed? Hundreds? Thousands?"

"None since you left!" she defended. "I wanted to be good enough for you. *Honorable.* That boy has had the benefit of your goodness his entire life and he *still* became the thing your sister feared. I've seen first hand what the Nephilim are capable of and once they turn, I'm telling you, there is *no* saving them. *Call your sister.*"

"You told me your children were taken from you. Did you mean vampires, or did you have real kids, before?"

"Why would you hurt me with that question?"

"What would you do, if he was yours? What *wouldn't you do* to help your kid?"

She thought about her daughters and the resentment she still felt for not being able to watch them grow up. Wyatt would never forgive her if she didn't let him try, so, she stepped aside, allowing him to open the door. As he walked out, she followed closely behind, unwilling to let him face this danger alone.

"I need you," Will quavered, tears spilling over his cheeks.

Michelle pulled him into the apartment and hugged him tightly. "What happened?" she asked, closing the door and looking him over. "How are your wounds gone?"

"My dad, he…I don't know where to start."

"Okay. Why don't tell me how you got hurt?"

"A pack of wolves attacked me in my backyard. I had it coming."

"Why did they--"

"Because I killed one of their--" he struggled to get the rest out. "One of their kids."

"You what?"

"A four-year-old kid. He bit someone I cared about and turned him into-- it doesn't matter. I should've gone home. I should've let it go, but that night, after the bowling alley, I was so angry. I couldn't calm down. I tried to stop, but I couldn't control it. I couldn't--"

"Oh, God, Will."

"That's just the beginning. I killed the whole pack when they came for me. I almost killed the pizza guy. Michelle, I killed," he stopped himself, afraid to say it out loud, the realness of the words in his head like a knife to his heart.

"Who?"

"I didn't mean to," he sobbed. "I swear, I didn't."

"Will, who was it?"

He wiped the tears from his face and with a trembling voice told her, "Michelle, I killed my grandfather."

"Jesus, Will."

He broke down, taking her in his arms and pulling her down with him as he fell to his knees. He cried into her shoulder, holding her so tightly that it hurt. She was a lifeboat in a sea of chaos, the only thing that made sense to him anymore. She pet his hair and rubbed his back, tears forming in her own eyes as her greatest fear was being realized. "Okay," she settled, knowing what she had to do. "Okay, why don't you get yourself cleaned up and I'll make us something to eat and we can figure out what to do next, all right?"

He nodded, getting up and walking towards the bathroom, the blood on his clothes leaving Michelle's shirt and carpet stained. Once she was sure he was in the bathroom, she took out her phone and texted Gabriel everything she'd just heard. It destroyed her to do it, the pit in her stomach urging her not to. But, it was the right thing.

Will was out of control and had to be stopped. She rubbed the tears from her eyes and as she hit send, she could feel him behind her.

"Gabriel?!" he shouted. "You told my aunt?! Do you know what she'll do to me?!"

"I'm worried about you," she cried, spinning around to face him. "What you've done, it's--"

"Did she send you?" he accused. "Did you come here to spy on me? Was any of this...were we real for you?"

"Of course we're real, Will. I love you. I love you so much. Nothing that happened between us was fake, not since--"

"Since?"

"I wasn't supposed to like you. I was supposed to work at the donut shop, watch from a distance, pop up where you happened to be once in a while, like at the SATs."

"You knew who I was?"

"Yeah, but I didn't recognize you at the shop. I didn't know you'd grown like that. I just thought you were a hot guy trying to ask me out. But, when you told me your name--"

"You went out with me, anyway? Knowing what I was? You do know, right? That I'm a freak? A monster?"

"You're not," she whimpered. "You're not a monster to *me*. When that tornado came through and you let me in, you were so kind to me. No one had ever treated me like that before. No one ever saw me the way you did. I fell for you that day."

"You fell for me, and now you're sentencing me to death. You love me, but you'd let me *die*?"

"I don't really think she'd kill you. She loves you."

"She *will* kill me. She will. She knows what I'm turning into. And, the thing is, I don't blame her. She's not wrong."

"You're a good person, Will. She knows that. I'll tell her--"

"So, you did see, didn't you? The night at the bowling alley. You saw what I did to that guy."

"Yeah."

"Why didn't you call her *then*?" he barked. "I was slipping. You could've prevented *all* of this."

"Because I'm in love with you. I didn't want to lose you. If there was a chance--"

"Does it look to you like there's a chance?" he yelled, grabbing a knife from the kitchen drawer. "Do I look like someone that can be saved?" He held the blade to his throat. "Is this what I deserve? Because this is what she'll do."

"Put the knife down."

"Don't worry, this can't kill me. It'll just put me down long enough that I won't be able to hurt anyone else until my aunt gets here. Or maybe you can do it yourself? You have a tub, right?"

"Stop," she sobbed.

"You can drag me in, hold my head under. Take the knife with you, in case I struggle. Stab me in the heart. That should knock me out long enough for you to get the job done."

"Stop it, Will," she begged, taking the knife from his hand and throwing it to the floor.

"How could you do this to me?" he sniffled. "You're the only girl I've ever loved and you broke my heart."

"I won't let her kill you," she promised. "I'll tell her--"

"You can't stop *her*. Do you know what she is? My dad told me about her powers. She can do *anything*. She's a force of nature."

"She's your aunt. She won't--"

"She's an angel first, above everything else, and she's coming to kill me, thanks to you."

"No, Will," She took his hands, but he pushed her away, a bolt of lightning exploding from his hands to hers. She fell, her body shaking violently on the floor, her eyes glazed over, her mouth foaming. She went still, her vacant eyes staring into nothing.

"Michelle," Will whimpered, kneeling beside her. "Michelle, please," He checked for a pulse, but there was none. He listened for her breath and heartbeat. Nothing. He fell back, new tears pouring down his cheeks. He buried his face in his hands. There was nothing for him left in the world. Without her, he was lost. Loneliness filled him like hot chocolate on a cold night, it's comfort strange, but right somehow. He stood, listening to the thunder clap outside, the flashes of lightning brightening the dimly lit apartment. *This is it*, he thought. *This is who I'm meant to be.*

Chapter 28

"Bitch, what the fuck?!" Valerie snapped as Gabriel and Lucifer entered the apartment. "You left your phone. I saw *all* that shit. Why didn't you tell me there was a fucking Ne--"

"Lucifer, go to your room," Gabriel ordered.

He guffawed.

"Please, go."

"All right," he acquiesced, intrigued. As Gabriel led Valerie to the sofa, Lucifer quietly stole the phone from the counter and took it to the hall where he stayed, out of sight, but well within earshot. He scrolled through the texts as he listened, growing more and more agitated as he read.

"Tae's niece?!" Valerie screeched. "You sent that poor girl to do *your* dirty work?"

"Tae told her who I was, *what* I was. She was the only person I could trust that Barachiel wouldn't recognize. She was just supposed to watch and report back. If he started showing signs, I--"

"You what?"

"I would have handled it."

"You would've killed him? Wyatt's son? Fuck, bitch, hasn't that boy been through enough?"

"Obviously. That's why I didn't kill him when he was a baby. I almost did. After B took him away, I went to his house when he was asleep. I snuck in, stood over Will's crib. I was gonna drown him in the sink, dry him off, try to make it look like SIDS. But B would've been devastated." Tears fell from Gabriel's eyes, something Valerie had never seen before. "He'd just lost his wife and, God, Uri, the look on his face when I couldn't bring her back. It broke me. He was *gutted*. This kid gave him hope, something to live for. If I took that from him, I don't know that he would've recovered. So, I checked in, visited a few times a year, talked to B every couple of days to make sure everything was all right. And, when Will started going out into the world, I sent Michelle. I had her in martial arts classes so she could defend herself, just in case, and I made it very clear that it was too dangerous to get friendly. Casual acquaintances tops. Nothing else."

"Well, she must not have listened, since he was at her place. That poor girl's probably dead, along with a kid and Wyatt's dad. His *dad*."

"Will's fucked up," Gabriel worried. She glanced up toward the hallway, knowing her brother had been listening the entire time. "That whole town's in danger. Southport, Indiana better lock its doors and close its windows because if he's half as nutty as I think he is, there's gonna be hell to pay."

Lucifer slunk to his bedroom and opened the window, rage coloring his face like rouge. He climbed out and took off, determined to make this right.

Wyatt drove down the dark road, the too-few street lights little help in seeing through the downpour. "Wyatt, look out!" Allydia yelped, able to see the figure lurking in the middle of the street. He slammed on the breaks, the car sliding and drifting sideways before coming to a stop. The man approached and soon, in the brightness of the headlights, they could make out who it was.

"Lucifer," Wyatt commanded, exiting the car, not bothering to close the door. "Go home!"

"You know I can't do that, brother. Not after what you've set upon us."

"Did Gabriel send you?"

"No, our sister is feeble when it comes to you. She believes the loss of someone else you love may drive you mad. I suspect she's right, but in your heart, you know what must be done."

Wyatt stepped closer, getting directly in Lucifer's face. "You leave my son alone."

"Have you any idea what he's done?" Lucifer barked back. "He killed a family of shifters, a four-year-old child, and your father."

Wyatt backed off, his stomach falling. "You're lying."

"I'm not. Gabriel's spy told her. I read the messages myself. A girl named Michelle."

"Gabriel *planted* her?"

"Of course. She may put your delicate feelings above her common sense, but she's not *stupid*. Now, it seems your progeny has killed the girl, as well. I overheard Gabriel telling Uriel all about your offspring's misadventures. She'll be a tad cross with me when I return, but I trust she'll understand. She learned long ago to put what's right ahead of her emotions."

Suddenly, the boom of an explosion rang out in the distance. They could see plumes of smoke rising from the center of town and the orange glow of flames tinting the sky above. Overhead, several lightning bolts stretched across the overcast, heading in the same direction and, eventually, all coming down on buildings on the same block.

"I see he shares your flare for the dramatic as well as your powers," Lucifer quipped.

"Jesus Christ," Wyatt breathed.

"How many times must I ask that you not say--" Another explosion erupted, this one louder than the last. "I'm sorry, brother, but you know what I must do." Wyatt grabbed one of his arms to stop him, but Lucifer wrapped the other around him as if in an embrace. "Have it your way," he sighed. "You won't be the first person I've had along for a ride today." He carried Wyatt as he flew over the town, coming down hard on the sidewalk across from Pine's, now engulfed in flames. The auto repair shop next door and several homes, too, were on fire, the rain of no help in putting out the blaze that lit up the street so well, it was as if there were a spotlight on the block.

"Dad?" Will called, emerging from around the corner, his shirt singed and his demeanor off.

"Hello, nephew," Lucifer greeted.

"Who's this?" Will wondered, crossing the street to meet them.

"What did you do?" Wyatt asked through the tears that mingled with rain on his cheeks.

"I saw it on a show," Will explained. "If I destroy the town, everyone will leave. They'll be safe and I can stay, alone. I'm too dangerous to be around people. It's the right thing to do."

"You're killing people."

"That's what I'm telling you. I'm unsafe. I killed that kid that turned Arthur into that thing, the pack that came for revenge,"

"And my father?" Wyatt asked, his voice breaking.

"That was an accident," Will insisted. "I just wanted to meet him, see if we looked alike. But, he thought I was a burglar, called the cops. I told him who I was, but he didn't believe me. He just kept yelling at me to leave. When I wouldn't, he grabbed me, pushed me, and I...it just came out of me, like instinct. The electricity in his heart, I sped it up. I didn't mean to, I swear. When he let me go and my mind cleared and I realized what I was doing, I stopped, but...he fell down."

Wyatt covered his mouth as he sobbed, the awfulness of what he was hearing too much to take.

"I tried to save him," Will continued. "I tried to restart his heart, but nothing happened. I called nine-one-one. I didn't know what else to do."

"How did you get into the city?"

"It's only a two and a half hour flight. I slipped some antihistamine in your drink with dinner and snuck out. You're already a heavy sleeper. It was easy."

"You drugged me?"

"You wouldn't have let me go. To be honest, I'm surprised you're so upset."

"Surprised?!"

"You think I don't know how miserable that man made you? I do. I remember everything Mom thought about while I was in her. At college, the booze, the drugs, the suicide attempts. *Three times* you tried to *end it* because of him. He was a dick that made your life such hell that you didn't want it anymore. But no amount of pills can kill things like us, right? Only one thing can kill me." He held his hands out and let the rain fall through his fingers. "And only one thing can kill you. Is that why you bailed on the Bar exam and started Leroy Jenkins-ing into burning buildings? Were you trying to *die?*"

"That's enough," Lucifer growled.

"Seriously, who *are* you?" Will inquired.

"I'm your dear uncle, come to end this madness once and for all." He rushed toward him, reaching for his collar, but Will threw a bolt of lightning, sending Lucifer flying through the window of a house behind him.

"Wyatt!" Allydia called, running toward them. Will knocked her back with a ball of electricity, rendering her unconscious on the pavement.

"You have to stop this," Wyatt pleaded. "I don't want to hurt you."

"It's okay, Dad," Will said, hugging his father. The two cried there for several seconds in the rain before Will spoke into Wyatt's ear. "I know it would devastate you to hurt me. Don't worry. You won't have to." He squeezed him tight and let the full power of his soul loose, white lightning pouring from him like a river through a broken levy into Wyatt's torso. He shook, his heart exploding, blood oozing from his mouth, nose, and ears. The heat was so intense, it melted his skin before his body caught flame. Will let him go, watching sadly as he fell, a heap of little more than charred bone.

"WYATT!" Allydia screamed, scrambling to her feet and racing toward them. Lucifer staggered from the house, livid, his eyes set on his monstrous nephew. Allydia collapsed to her knees in the road, the flames too high for her to get near. She wailed, the sorrow unlike anything she'd felt before.

"Who are you?" Will shouted at Lucifer from afar.

"Your ignorance is insulting," Lucifer huffed. "No matter. Soon, you'll be in Purgatory, left alone in the cold and dark to think about the terrible things you've done. When your time is served, I hope your next life sees you more stable. If not, I'll meet you there, as well."

"Lucifer," Will realized. He backed away and started to run. Lucifer stood over Wyatt's burning corpse, the knowledge that there was nothing he could do to save him inciting in him a feeling of despondency, an emotion he hadn't felt in centuries. He took a deep breath and crossed the street, walking past the smoldering donut shop, following Will into the woods. It was darker there, harder to see, but he navigated his way through the trees and brush, more determined than ever to end the destruction caused by the abomination he called 'nephew'. He could hear the boy in the distance, snapping twigs and rustling leaves as he made his escape, but just as Lucifer was sure of which way to go, he was halted in his tracks by the feeling of something familiar. He turned, and there, standing among the trees, was his brother. Not Wyatt, but the Barachiel he remembered, looking just as he had in Norway all those years ago.

"Barachiel? How is this possible? You should be home."

"The vampire," the angel explained. "She fed on me once, taking so much blood, it became part of her DNA. Had I been human, I would have perished that day. I'm trapped here, until the Gates open, as long as she lives."

"Would you like me to kill her? Set you free?"

"Thank you, but, no. There's more work to do. Gabriel will fill you in. I'll heal my body and return to it, once I've ended this. It was nice getting a chance to speak with you without my human filter. Being Wyatt has been difficult. There's a disconnect between us, the human brain being so fragile. I appreciate you coming to protect me. How does it feel, doing my job?"

"Burdensome."

Barachiel laughed.

"Why did you do it?" Lucifer queried. "Why did you bring a *Nephilim* into the world?"

"As Wyatt, I was so in love with Annie that not much else mattered. I could feel her pulling away. She was frightened of me. She had prayed for a baby before things got bad, and I thought if I gave her one, she'd stay with me. Turns out, though, the baby was the thing that took her away. You have to understand how muddled the human mind is. Reason is often ignored. I'm not myself when I'm him. I wish we had more time, but when Wyatt has a natural death, we will be together again, I'm guessing for a hundred and forty years before we go above and below. It'll be good to catch up. As for now, though, I have a mess that needs tending to. If you'll excuse me."

"Let me do this for you, brother. Please. You shouldn't have to--"

"He's my Thryme," Barachiel maintained, disappearing into the night, his true form pure energy, unencumbered by the constraints of matter. Lucifer sighed and headed in the direction Will had been running in.

Will sat on the soggy ground, the storm having passed and the fireflies floating by, reminding him of the night he and Michelle had spent there. He was alone now, as it always should have been. He could finally breathe, knowing there was no one left for him to hurt.

"I'm sorry I let this happen," Barachiel apologized, appearing before him, his blond hair and cobalt eyes striking, even in the moonlight. "I shouldn't have been so careless."

"Who are you?" Will asked, getting to his feet.

"You really are so much like me. Well, not *me*, but, the *other* me."

Will studied the man's face and looked into his eyes. Then, it occurred to him. "Bara--"

Barachiel grasped the boy's throat and lifted him off the ground. Will tried electrocuting him, but his bolts went right through him.

"I really am sorry," Barachiel lamented as he carried Will closer to the creek and slammed him down into it. The boy thrashed, struggling to get free, unable to get hold of any part of the angel. "You're fundamentally good. Wyatt's influence, no doubt. It's your physiology that's the problem. You will get another chance and when you do, I will help guide you to be the best version of yourself. Remember, child, that you are loved."

As Will's body went limp, Barachiel waved goodbye to the soul that drifted off to its next destination. He placed the body on the ground and smoothed the hair away from the boy's closed eyes.

"Are you all right, brother?" Lucifer asked as he approached. "That must have been--"

"Once I'm Wyatt, I won't remember," Barachiel told him. "You should tell me. I might need to be watched to make sure I don't do something rash, but I'd much rather know the truth than think he did this to himself. Promise me."

"I will do what's right, Barachiel. I swear it."

Allydia continued to weep, her face pressed to Wyatt's exposed ribs. His top half was nothing more than bones and ash, still warm from the fire that had gone out just moments before. She put her hand to his forehead, but the skull crumbled at the touch. She wailed again, her heartbreak all-encompassing. As she cried, the smell of blood drifted up from the corpse. A warm wetness on her cheek forced her eyes open and she couldn't believe what she was seeing. Muscle and organs formed, a heart appeared and began to beat, the skull reformed, skin covering it. Soon, he was again whole, the lover she thought she'd lost. His eyes flew open as he took what felt like his first breath.

"Wyatt," she whispered, astonished and grateful. "Wyatt!" She held him in her arms as he sat upright, inhaling the sweet smell of his skin and bathing herself in his body heat, the most perfect warmth in existence.

"Where is he?" he asked, shakily standing.

"He went into the woods, but, Wyatt, your brother went after him."

Wyatt barreled through the forest, his instincts telling him in which direction to run. Allydia followed, dodging tree branches and tripping hazards as she went. As the sound of the rushing creek grew louder, so did Wyatt's dread. His chest tightened and his heart pounded as he felt something entirely foreign to him...fear.

They came to a clearing and there, on the edge of the creek, was Will's body, wet and still, sinking into the mud beneath him.

"No, no, no, no," Wyatt repeated, hurrying to his son's side. He began CPR, giving thirty chest compressions followed by a breath. "Wake up," he sobbed, starting more chest compressions. "Please. Please, wake up." But there was no life left to save. Allydia placed a sympathetic hand on Wyatt's back as he scooped the boy up in his arms and wept, his lungs feeling as if they could not take in air. The vampire wrapped her arms around his shoulders and kissed the back of his head as he grieved.

"You should run," she warned, feeling Lucifer approach them from behind the trees. Wyatt looked up and saw him there, a pained expression on his face.

"I'm sorry, brother," Lucifer said quietly.

"I don't know how," Wyatt swore through tears and strained breaths. "But I *will* kill you for this."

"I expect you'll try. I can't blame you, I understand. If *you'd* murdered someone *I--*"

"*I said run*," Allydia ordered.

"Very well," Lucifer complied, flying off, leaving Wyatt to mourn, unwilling to break his brother's heart further with the truth.

Chapter 29

Gabriel was a wreck. Feeling Wyatt die and come back had been an emotional roller coaster of devastation, physical pain, and relief. She was confused as to how he'd returned but was so grateful that he had that she almost thanked God before remembering that He couldn't hear her. She anxiously paced around the living room while Valerie took a late-night nap on the couch.

"Oh, shit," Gabriel muttered, rushing toward the door.

"What?" Valerie asked, popping up from her slumber.

"Be nice," she instructed, opening the door. Lucifer came in, his face ashen, despair in his eyes. Gabriel threw her arms around him, cradling the back of his neck with her right hand. He hugged her back, allowing her to comfort him as a single tear made its way down his cheek.

"We must let him believe it," he said into his sister's hair. She nodded, tears in her eyes now, too.

Michelle rolled over, wiping the drool from her mouth as she stood, her skin tingling and her head feeling heavy. She stumbled through the kitchen where she opened the freezer door and took out a frozen pizza box. She reached her hand inside and pulled out the bag of human blood she'd been hiding there and tossed it in the microwave. "Won't need *you* anymore," she sighed, taking the vial of Hattie's blood from the fridge and dropping it in the trash. The timer beeped and she emptied the contents of the plastic medical bag into a glass and drank greedily. She licked the blood from her lips and picked up her phone, dialing Hattie's number and holding the cell to her ear.

"Plan V in full effect," she told her friend when she answered. "Thanks for saving me."

"Are you sure this is what you want?" Hattie asked. "It's not an easy life, being what we are."

"It's better than being dead."

"What other secrets have you been keeping?" Lucifer asked, standing at the bar, taking a sip of Earl Grey as the sun rose, neither of them having yet been to bed.
"Barachiel told me there's more for us to do."

"A ton more," Gabriel confirmed. "We're not even *kind of* done. You think Lilith was just a distraction. She wasn't. She started something when she was here, something I've been prepping for *for years.*"

"Do tell."

"You're gonna want to sit down."

The End

The Complete Seventh Day Series

Seraphim
Nephilim
Elohim
Cain
Alukah
Coven
Sinclair

Printed in Great Britain
by Amazon